SOUL RESIN

for Dianne—
Hope it's as good
as Rick's
[signature] '02

SOUL RESIN

by C.W. Cannon

FC2

Normal/Tallahassee

Published by FC2 with support provided by Florida State Univer-
sity, the Unit for Contemporary Literature of the Department of
English at Illinois State University, the Program for Writers of the
Department of English of the University of Illinois at Chicago, the
Illinois Arts Council, and the Florida Arts Council of the Florida
Division of Cultural Affairs

Address all inquiries to: Fiction Collective Two, Florida State
University, c/o English Department, Tallahassee, FL 32306-
1580

ISBN: Paper, 1-57366-099-X

Library of Congress Cataloging-in Publication Data

Cannon, C. W. (Charles W.)
 Soul resin / C.W. Cannon.-- 1st ed.
   p. cm.
 ISBN 1-57366-099-X
 1. New Orleans (La.)--Fiction. 2. Immortalism--Fiction. I.
Title.
 PS3603.A54 S68 2002
 813'.6--dc21

                                        2001005721

Cover Design: Victor Mingovits
Book Design: Amanda Karvelaitis and Tara Reeser

Produced and printed in the United States of America
Printed on recycled paper with soy ink

Acknowledgement of Sources

I am indebted to a few books in particular for my vision of Reconstruction in New Orleans. In addition to George Washington Cable, I should acknowledge the following works: John Blassingame's *Black New Orleans*, Eric Foner's *Reconstruction: America's Unfinished Revolution*, James Gill's *Lords of Misrule: Mardi Gras and the Politics of Race*, and Arnold Hirsch and Joseph Logsdon's *Creole New Orleans: Race and Americanization* (especially Logsdon and Caryn Cosse Bell's essay, "Americanization of Black New Orleans"). Particular credit should go to Georges Vandal's *Anatomy of a Catastrophe: the New Orleans Riot of 1866*, from which I derived my anatomy of said riot. Many of the public statements printed in my fictional account are in fact the same statements reported by different newspaper accounts of the time (I changed the names of the speakers)—I have these accounts from Vandal, in which the real speakers are identified.

I received critical advice from historian Eric Arnesen, of the University of Illinois at Chicago, author of *Waterfront Workers of New Orleans: Race, Class, and Politics 1863-1923*.

For Laura

"And the Watchman said, 'The morning cometh, and also the night.'"

Isaiah 21.12

November 23. Like Farragut's gunboats and Hurricane Betsy, it came up the river. Still miles away, the approaching trident blasts woke people all over the city. They rushed out of their homes, some still in bedclothes, some dressed and armed. Irrational behavior set in. People began shooting at each other, then wildly in all directions, only finally to turn the gun on themselves. Out of some buried instinct from a former era, thousands flocked to the levee. There they saw the Mississippi rising, rising, then overflowing: as if a single bather were joined by too many guests, the river's trough had no more room for water. It began in snaking little rivulets, then lunged over in great messy splashes.

But the flooding was the least of it. Well before the river reached its boiling point, onlookers saw the ominous shapes floating round the bend at what used to be called Slaughterhouse Point. Great black clouds like great black ships, the palpable warp in the air oozed itself into the harbor and then began reaching out in all directions. Like a great neighing black horse's head it came down out of the sky as quickly as it had dug itself out of the earth.

11

Some dead came back for revenge. Other dead cast their lot with the living, out of principle. Many of the living volunteered for the opposition, suicide was their badge of honor. The dead fared the worst. Countless ranks of them ended up in eternity's tarpit, what we now know to call Soul Resin.[1]

---

[1] Charles Cannon, *Soul Resonance: A History of the Great Rift and Its Consequences for the Living and the Dead*

November 21

Mills Loomis Mills

Yesterday was a day like any other but tomorrow won't be. That's what I'm telling myself to psych up for taking the leap. I'm about ready because all those yesterdays piling up are starting to get pretty tiresome. Even my run-ins with the police don't give me a rise anymore. Had one yesterday, had one today. The law and me bump into each other a lot because my research involves recently dead or dying bleeding bodies. Found a doozy this morning. I was attentively sucking up that blood-smell, and listening, but minding my own business and not touching anything. Until the cop showed up and got on my shit for snooping around his hallowed crime scene. I had a lot more use for it than he did, but, as usual, when I told him that he got aggressive on me. Gripped his maglite and asked me if I "wanted to get my head busted."

Heard that before, right? But I'm not surprised they all use the same expressions, considering they all do the same thing over and over again, day in day out. They do so much of it I bet their dreams are crowded with it, too, which means they'll never get anywhere, really. The dream is the door, but if it's clogged up with going over the shit you did that day and "working it

out," as the shrinks put it, you'll never find the door-
knob.

Luckily, this cop wasn't too observant. I was looking in through the window for quite a while before he
noticed me, so I saw plenty. Victim was pantsless, legs
on the bed, butt in the air (something stuck up it, too—
looked like one of those Club Anti-theft Auto devices).
Fat guy, pretty unattractive, judging from the backside.
His torso was leaning to the floor, arms down there,
too, and head, I couldn't see them from my angle.
Didn't matter, though, I already knew they cut his hands
off. Probably made mojo tokens with them. I could
tell the hands were not on the premises—and I
would've told the cop, if he wasn't such a dickhead.
See, when a bloodway is severed, the squeak of the
spilling blood emits something like a question which
should be answered in kind from what used to be its
destination. The hands didn't answer. Missing. I knew
all this from my nose and ears. Eyes are more often a
crutch than a help, that's one reason the cops never
get anywhere in their investigations.

I've had a long day. I wasn't planning on surveying
a crime scene, but the yelping bloodcells woke me
up, and I figured it would be a good warm-up for the
main event. Like stretching. I hate sleeping at night,
it's such a waste (I mean real sleep, where you just let
the dreams go by without getting involved). But I made
myself do it last night so I'd be alert for this bayou
cruise. Yep, bayou cruise! On the Mississippi Belle.
I'm laughing, too, but I've got my reasons. There's
souls in them there swamps! And the stuff that didn't
quite make soul, which is what I'm after. After the cop
chased me off I had just enough time to stroll over to
the steamboat landing and sit around on a bench for
hours waiting for the suckers to show up, watching
stray cats and people go through garbage until cops

on mountain bikes shooed them all off. I pretended to be reading a newspaper, so they left me alone (oh, yeah, and I'm white). Then the big busses pulled up and they all got out and lined up to get their tickets. With every one of them paying with credit cards and dragging out the coupons they clipped from the tourist books in their motels the night before, it took forever. I bought a ticket with the last cash I had and walked up the plank with the others. Everyone seemed suspicious that I was alone, so I irritated them by standing too close and asking them questions. Where were they from? Did they like New Orleans? Was it their first visit? I told them I was working on a story for a local locals' magazine about how to best serve them.

Then the Belle started inching away from her landing. It's a sternwheeler, and the funny thing is that the paddle turns round and round even though they don't need it anymore. First thing everybody did after walking up the gangway, even before they started shelling out for souvenirs to remember the thing they hadn't even done yet, was go astern and stare over the edge at the paddle and take pictures of it like it was a pink gorilla.

One way to keep from getting bored: if you look at people like you look at a TV show, life's always entertaining. These tourists lining up with their cameras to go downriver and take pictures of pollution and outright garbage. Thirty bucks! Reading the police report's free. Getting the information before it gets printed is even freer (and funner, and more productive). But see, it's not these people's function in history to do something like that, so it's OK. That's what I tell myself.

And I'm scared, too, I'll be honest. This thing I'm gonna do has obviously never been done before. Risks involved. Dangerous. Socially unacceptable. But definitely it's the next logical step in the march of progress, even though that might not be a good thing. Still, that's

17

what people do. They keep going ahead and that's the march of civilization. Borders must be expanded. This time it's me or nobody, so it's me.

But I've got cold feet and I'm naturally lazy—not my fault, the way I was raised—so don't blame me for enjoying life a little bit along the way. Like a fine day on the old steamboat and the sun and breeze and smell of popcorn and sticky soda-syrup underfoot. They also had these cool stormclouds, lurking, and the other big boats— industrial style—and the multi-colored wharves, each named after a street. Like a movie with the screen all around, but too bad the characters were dressed all wrong. Don't get me wrong, though, I'm not a nostalgist—I know better than that. If I was on this steamboat when it was a real one, I would have been shoveling coal (at least I wouldn't have been getting sold off of it). No, I think the best things have ever been is right now—safe and fake as opposed to real and evil. Everybody dressed in shorts and t-shirts and sunglasses, instead of the eighteen layers of clothing in the sun that made people stink so bad and get sick and die back in the good old days.

Everybody was drinking hurricanes in those plastic hourglass cups. They're red drinks so I had one, too (not blood-red, though, a fakey neon red).

The motto for cameras was "use 'em if y'got 'em." The poor people that didn't have a camera (mostly kids) watched the people holding the cameras. So nobody had to look at anything they didn't know without looking through an expensive lens—except me and the help, of course. The help watched the customers. I watched the riverbanks. Big iron workaholic sick-looking ships getting worked by cranes. Wharves wharves wharves, all sagging, with flat warehouses called Piety, Independence, Poland and other bullshit, all painted different pastelly shades of blue, yellow, orange. Men coming in and out of them, sometimes driving forklifts. Working for a living. All got their pictures snapped. Then big box frames for shipbuilding, tugs looking square as bad suburban houses, pushing black barges. If anybody saw the shiny rainbow-colored grease spots on the water, they kept it to themselves. They were all looking for gators, though, and they didn't get any.

The biggest kick for me was going in between the big tankers parked downriver from the city waiting to come in and unload. Some dumb kid started crying to his mom about how they were spaceships come to get him. The mom was clueless, too, though, because she didn't feel the fear at all, and the fear *was* there, just not where the kid thought. That's why I was out there. But it wasn't the manned functioning tankers and barges and tugs sending it out for me to smell. Obviously, it was the gone ships doing that, and their crews.

I don't resent the people that don't know, though, that can't feel. That was me for most of my short life, and, well, that's "normal", anyway. It's been a long road with lots of twists and turns, and the river has its bend, etc. I started off like most people, going through the motions of what an old teacher of mine (the only one I liked) would call "the expectations of my social class," or some shit. Yeah, I went to college. Up at L.S.U. Half my time in the sleepy classroom and the better half on or around the levee. I joined a party frat, kept up a B average, coulda been a lawyer! But I'm so glad things happened differently. If a lawyer was out here on this river, he'd be thinking about how much the live ships cost to manufacture, and how long they probably have to wait before they can come in and unload, maybe even how deep the river might be at this or that bend. It bores me just to think about it and when my mind turns to that kind of mechanical thought-cycling, I don't know whether to cry for them or holler for me. Lawyers, engineers, "professors," even

19

preachers, they never smell anything except food and waste—animal and industrial—and the substitutes they've invented for crotch (which other animals still dig).

Well, maybe history professors are a little different. They might know how a certain smell got there, for example. And the good ones—yeah, like Professor Vidrine, who sort of got me into this mess—they know the one important fact: the blood has been shed (they just don't know what to do with it).

But a lawyer will never know. They never know anything unless they see a number attached to it. A lawyer will never smell the core of a night's darkness and the blood and its coy lisping whispers there and what it can do. Like on this very river that they make so much money off they can't hear the voice of its hidden life.

Rafe Vidrine, from Discriminate Mob: The American Race Riot, 1863-1992

We have seen in what various ways the New York City Draft Riot of 1863 can be counted as America's first modern race riot. Perhaps its principal defining feature was the displacement of a complex set of enmities and legitimate reasons for complaint onto a brutal distillation of racist rage. In this case anti-war and labor frustrations drove an immigrant white working-class mob to shoot, hang, bludgeon, and burn alive scores of black New Yorkers. Also, like many a case of mass racial violence after it, it took place during high summer.

New Orleans' turn would come exactly three years later, in July of 1866. But aside from the almost identical weather, it would differ in almost every respect. A major distinction was that the carnage at New Orleans on July 30 was more directly *political violence*, that is to say, politics was not a sub-text, but, as in the case of many a European urban uprising, the mob action was from the beginning planned and supervised by political parties. What distinguished it, though, from similar European incidents—1830, 1848, 1871—was that the violence was instigated by reactionary rather than revolutionary forces. For America it would be significant as the harbinger of the political terror that would eventually destroy Reconstruction and re-chain the South to the same oligarchs who had managed the splendid catastrophe of the Civil War.

A leading New Orleans radical, Thomas J. Durant, had earlier warned those oligarchs of the revolutionary forces unwittingly unleashed by themselves. During a speech to the Workingmen's National Union League on December 3, 1863, Durant spoke of how the slaveocrats had precipitated the war and now had to endure far greater changes in the society than would have been thinkable had they not so fatally overestimated their own power. They had blundered themselves into a revolutionary situation and "revolutions never leave nations as they find them." The determination of the ex-Confederate elites to see that the revolution spawned by the inner Civil War and Reconstruction leave as little trace as possible on the political landscape of their fiefdom was precisely the cause of the thirty-four deaths of July 30. But such an outburst, or, more correctly put, *demonstration* (i.e. flexing of muscle) was long in coming and subject to many twisting levels of psychological and political preparation. The most strikingly decisive trend in the years leading up to the riot was the rapid raising of the defeated classes' expectations. Nash Newton Bascomb would write in his memoirs of 1889, "from the seemingly impenetrable night of 1864, like the lantern of a rescuing lightship drawing nearer through thick fog, we quickly realized that despite our wounds we would shout once more that the land was ours, that we and our fathers had shed blood for it and that the last limb of the last man would wield the sword in defense of our right as Louisianians, and as white men."

Bascomb was, of course, influential in the depredations of 1866, just as he was behind the coup attempt that was the Liberty Place "riot" of 1874. During the decade of his final triumph, the 1880s, he would help to fashion the New South of the "Redeemers," thus laying the groundwork for the South that would prevail well into the next century. We can see 1866 as the first cautious step of a badly bruised but miraculously resurgent (and very small) social stratum bent on domination.

Thirty-four deaths, among which at least five could be called planned political assassinations, may not seem "cautious" unless we remind ourselves of the casualties of the before and after of the period, that is, the Civil War and the twenty-year lynching campaign following Reconstruction—a rear guard action carried out by the same terrorist secret societies formed by men like Bascomb in 1866 and subsequent years.

New York in 1863 leaped ahead to foreshadow later clashes (East St. Louis, 1908; Chicago, 1919), but the period in between would witness the model set by New Orleans. Unlike later, mostly Northern, racial rioting, the Southern riots of the Reconstruction period also featured murders—assassinations—of prominent white radical political figures. The shifting political realignments during Reconstruction moved more like a wrecking-ball than a pendulum. Against every intransigence of the planter "rebel" element, the radicals would fling increasing rhetorical vehemence and call for bolder policies restricting the power of their opponents—who had, after all, been defeated in war. The slaveocrat class would then respond with ever increasing violence. After the failure of their more conventional civil war, they resorted to underground terror tactics which did indeed prove much more effective and much less costly to them.

Mills Loomis Mills

No, historians are paper-pushers just like the rest of them. What was it Marx said, "We don't aim to write history, what we mean to do is change it"? That Professor Vidrine was fun to listen to, but like a joke is: no results. Easy platitudes. Outrage without a gun. But, you see, what I feel is not outrage. Outrage is a crutch, too. You can get all dramatic in some lecture, but how is that any different than making a side-show freak for tourists, like the Mississippi Belle, *look* like something that used to have a real function? The historian today doesn't have a real function, but that could change. The New Science will provide jobs for lots of people and professions that don't really have a use today. To really use history, the first thing is to get over the idea of books. The real thing is in the real people. So what kind of people are historians into? *The dead ones.* They'll never know them unless they stop reading about them and get out there and meet them.

Society needs in general to get over the antiquated idea that dead people have no responsibilities. They're the ones who got us into this mess, after all. But in dealing with them, there's one way that historians should stay the way they already have been: they should be scientific about it. Unsentimental, objective, impersonal. Social workers need not apply. And that part about leaving your heart at the door is hard, it was a hard-learned lesson for me.

I used to be all roly-poly and cuddly and feely-feely. Let things get to me too much, good and bad. Had a girlfriend (a fine and busty petite redhead who fucking loved me and loved fucking me).

Had a dog, too.

But now I know that love of another warm human or canine body is not the kind that matters. The New Science has freely absorbed tenets of the great religions. Among them is this: "there is a greater love"—and it's not about fucking people. But back then I was a regular sweet helpful boy who got along with everybody and was a little lazy. Therefore stoned all the time. I liked people so much, my favorite thing was to hang around and party with them all the day long. Me and my girlfriend were a real item. Everybody would say, "Mills and April, Mills and April, where's Mills and April!" Usually we'd be riding our bikes around or hanging out on the levee or in the batcher. We cut class all the time to be together and to be lazy—to be lazy together. We'd lay around in bed half the day, rolling all over each other. No lie. Not very productive.

April's people had a house down by Mandeville and sometimes we'd go down there. We rode our bikes all the way over there one time, jumped our bikes over the concrete ledge into Lake Ponchartrain and didn't give a damn. Four feet of warm muddy brown and not one wave. It was that time of year with dead fish floating around. But we didn't give a damn.

So we formalized things and got a dog and moved in together. If what happened to her had never happened, it's true, I could have ended up a lawyer complete with wife and babies (eventually I would have started going to class more). But "the river has its bend," and now me saying, "I'm glad she got killed" is not something I'd expect a regular person to understand. But when you get touched by a death (or maybe just the blood-spilling kind) you get a rare chance to see into it a little bit, over it, through it. At first all you get is a tiny little pinhole. Almost nothing, the kind of thing most people wouldn't even notice. It's a mood. One of those moods that's not happy or sad or angry or blue or high or namable in any way: never been catalogued before. Lots of people only get it when they're dreaming, anyway. They don't know what it is then, either. But it's the door, curtain, whatever. It's open just a crack, but you can nudge it a bit further. And they're all back there, billions and billions and billions of them.

But I wouldn't go looking for April, because her transient personality isn't worth much in the nasty cosmic scheme of things. Sounds cold, but hey. Too many of *us* for one to matter, much less them. You think it's crowded over here? You'll find out different when you take the trip.

Dear Mills,

Hey, I hear they're talking about you back at school! Yes, yes. Prof. LaVonne was out here (I told you about her, right?). I asked her if she knew any history people and told her you were my boyfriend and she said she was talking to Vidrine and he said you were quite a character! But she said he meant it in a good way. She's gonna be my advisor from now on back home. She says her and Vidrine are friends.

Speaking of back home, I'll be seeing you again very soon, lucky boy. Only two weeks! I better stop writing 'cause I'm getting horny just thinking about you. Remember you said you were gonna not jerk off for a while so you'd have a big load for my mouth? Better start getting dinner ready.

In love and lust,
April Do-Mae
XOXOXOX

Rafe Vidrine

I'm being stalked. I've gotten hang-up calls, strange postcards with no note or return address. The first one was a reproduction of an old *Harper's* magazine print depicting the distribution of rations after the Yankee take-over of New Orleans, under the porticoes of the Cabildo. Then came a few which were all old New Orleans scenes, either lithograph or old photos. The one I got today is the first to have a written message. The picture shows a participant in the Andalusian *Semana Santa*—his regalia strongly resembles a Klansman's—and was obviously intended to shock me, a black man (though the postcard was the first time in a month I'd thought of myself as such). The message on the back reads, "Our problems are older than we think."

I know who it is, and I'm not so much frightened as saddened. I'm actually relieved that it's not who I first suspected—I had worried that Mattie LaVonne's husband had finally gotten sick of our spending so much time together and stalking was his way to apply round-about pressure. But it dawned on me in my sleep last night who the real culprit is.

I had a student a couple of years ago who went off the deep end. I saw it coming. He wanted to be a history major, and his reasons were clear: he was in love with tales of gore and meanness and the history books are full of them. He had a snarl of conviction on his face at all times, just waiting for a suitable ideology to match it up with, for a cause to fire him up and get him rolling. The problem is, he never found one. He didn't have much in the way of a theory of history, but he knew what he liked in terms of specific details and periods. Reconstruction was a big favorite—that's how I ended up as his advisor. He told me he thought it would be a "fruitful period for research." I thought he meant they had a lot of newspapers then, and wrote a lot of letters. But he was talking about rope and gunpowder, of course. That's the kind of statistic he remembered best, the body count. He'd pipe up in class, "Three-hundred old people, women and children gunned down at Wounded Knee; 23,741 casualties in forty-eight hours at Shiloh; thirty-one blacks and three white radicals murdered at New Orleans, July 30, 1866."

But I doubt he ever read a book cover to cover. He was too distracted. Spaced-out, they used to say. Then he started dressing differently. That was the first outward sign of the edge creeping up on him. He started going in for this archaic look, bordering on costume. With no regard to weather he would come in those sultry broken-airconditioned lecture halls in heavy wool three-piece suits (out of season, of course). He had a watch chain, sometimes even a removable collar. Where did he get that stuff? I remember one day in particular, when my lecture had a greater impact on him than I would have wished.

It was a still, hot, humid day, I was delivering one of my tirades about how I know 'cause I come up in

Louisiana as a black man in the black belt way back when.
I told them about a regular case of a lynching, or a
"mysterious death," that is, more accurately, even
though I couldn't see much mysterious about it. The
name of the victim in this case was, yes, Lucius Holt.
(For some reason that name nags at me more than the
thousands of others.) Their assignment was to go back
into microfilm and find one of the stories about it from
the papers back then. I boomed out the issues in my
country preacher voice—that was my standard routine for A-level courses then: "Little Lucius was still yet
a boy, a child curious and promising in his faculties, if
not in his economic class and legal status. On a Saturday afternoon he went to make a delivery for the grocery store where he worked. That evening he went
missing. Only weeks later did they find his hanging
body out in some junk-dump in the swamps. What
insolence, what wrong glance brought him to this end?"

Then I quoted from Primo Levi, *If This Is a Man*—I
was on a comparative kick then—and that was it, end of
class. I shut my book and glared at them and turned my
back and walked out the door. But out the door I could
still feel the thickness of everybody's sweat from that
hall, the way it used to get wafted around from everybody fanning themselves with my syllabus, and then I
flashed on him: He'd been in there wearing an old-
timey three-piece suit with a tan Stetson and a short
wide 1930s tie.

The next day he tracks me down outside some other
class, and he's wearing the same outfit, only the tie seems
different, and he's breathing heavy—it must have been
ninety degrees. September. Back in antebellum times
they called it the "fever month." He says, "Professor
Vidrine, Professor Vidrine! I'm gonna figure it out! About
the real meaning of the events surrounding Lucius Holt's
disappearance and subsequent murder!"

I remember wondering, "Real meaning?! Have you not yet learned the real meaning of the history of this great nation? Have you not learned it from my lectures? What have you been smoking?" But before I could think of the diplomatic thing to say, he says, "Professor Vidrine, Professor Vidrine, I want to do a dissertation on it!"

"It? What? A boy named Lucius Holt who worked in a grocery store?"

He nodded and I started to do my job, be encouraging, make suggestions. "Well, yeah. You could find out more about Holt's family. Get down to the hall of records in Jefferson parish."

But then he says, "No, it's not about Lucius Holt, exactly, his particular case may not be what I'm interested in."

"What, lynching in general?" I asked him.

"Well, it may not be that the fact that it was, y'know, a lynching is that important either. I mean, what I need to find out is, like whether he bled a lot. You know if they did anything to him besides hang him?"

I just said, "I don't know, son," and started worrying right then.

Mills Loomis Mills

Actually, I think the dreams started before April made the move, but after, after I first heard the blood, they picked up and got more vivid, and then I eventually learned to focus them a little. After I moved down to New Orleans, that's when they really went ballistic. "City of a Million Dreams" is what the tune says and that's how many I started to have. I mean the kind when you're asleep and they don't even let you wake up. Like sitting alone in a dry sunlit afternoon room, or cell, sunbeams making the dust in the air pointy. Again and again, like the same room is like a series of them taking you down some hall.

Significant-feeling inexplicableness everywhere. These are the early stages, but then you start picking up the knowledge, if you have the endurance, the endurance to remember it all and hold it in your head throughout your waking hours. The knowledge that your surroundings are aware of your presence, then that the experiences you cherish as your own are not your own, after all. Whose are they?

Then the specific faces. Most people turn back at this point (if they ever even made it this far instead of lying about it). It takes stomach to see the whining faces of the dearly deceased in your dreams, people you don't even know. People you've never known blaming you for everything.

Anyway, the "Big Easy" is so crowded with hateful and bitter souls that the pilgrim is soon forced to hone his skills, perceive better, faster, tighter. Because the ghosts look and act like everyone else, in your dreams, or just on the street or at the grocery store. Sure, they're everywhere. You either feel it or you don't. If all I had to do was find the soul of an unhappily dead person, this would have been done before. And they're all openly pissed off about it. Who gets killed and likes it? No, they've all got complaints. They won't shut up about them. People killed by their spouses or their parents or their children. Ones tortured to death by strangers. You have to be able to shut these voices out and listen for the blood itself.

Yeah, it wouldn't take a Mills Loomis Mills to figure out that April's gotta be pissed as all hell, too, what they did to her. To tell the truth, I'd be sort of scared to meet her. She's probably figured out some way to blame me. Also, I've had to move on. I'm thinking about trying to, anyway. It's been awhile. There's other fish out there, though, live ones.

Hey Milly-Mill!

Remember how cool you felt when you took Vidrine's class and decided to be a history major? I think that's a pretty good example of how I feel now. I miss you, but I'm so glad I came out here. Sorry I whined so much about it before. Now I love it. New Mexico truly is the "Land of Enchantment." The only thing I'm sorry about is my mom copping out of getting you those tix to fly out here. Maybe you're right, I guess she doesn't like you. It's more like she doesn't trust you-or me-she thinks I won't study or do whatever she thinks I'm supposed to be doing out here if you're out here having fun with me. You'd love it out here, though. The neat thing is, it's like the opposite of home. Dry, not wet. Sandy, not muddy. Red and blue instead of green and brown. It's so spiritual out here, too, a different kind of spiritual than in the woods or on the levee. Oh, the stars! Anyway, it's beautiful and I wish you were here. AND-I'm gonna major in Native American Studies and come to grad. school out here! (If you marry me maybe I'll let you come with. OK maybe even if you don't marry me.)

The funny thing is I've finally gotten to know some Navajos, which is great, but that means I've also met a couple that hate white people. I guess there's mean stupid assholes everywhere, right? It's OK, 'cause it's worth it to meet the cool ones.

OK, dude, I love you and XXXOOO to 'Shoba. I know you're too lazy to write me, bummy-bum, but that's OK, I guess you're cute enough to get away with it. Anyway, you're thinking, only five more weeks, what's the point. See, I know how you think.

In love and lust,
April

Rafe Vidrine, from <u>Discriminate Mob: The American Race Riot, 1863-1992</u>

One might legitimately question whether the levels of active planning disqualify the violence of July 1866 from the heading of "riot," but only if one erroneously assumes that riots are "spontaneous." Riots are no more spontaneous than any other collective action. Leaving aside the nihilistic view that history is an indecipherable flurry of coincidences, we must assume that people shape events, and people make decisions. Riots happen at specific times, in response to specific and often concrete forces (i.e. hunger + evidence of abundance=bread riot); and there are always at least a handful of instigators. Furthermore, it is not only possible but imperative to name names in the effort to establish responsibility wherever pain is inflicted and lives are lost. In New Orleans, in the years after the Civil War, as throughout the South, one of the human forces shaping events remains even today largely cloaked in shadow—or, better put, under masks. We know of the Ku Klux Klan, of the Knights of the White Camelia, but these represent only two of many groups, two who never really intended to be "secret" societies.

Gov. James Madison Wells, finding himself in one of the great repeat acts of political history—the moderate who finds himself set upon by the rabid conservatives who elected him and whom he thought he could trust or control—alluded to the dangers of "secret associations" in his address to the new state legislature November 29, 1865. He may have known that members of such organizations sat before him, but he apparently did not know that many counted among his alleged supporters. The contempt of his listeners was rendered in mockery the following day, when N.N. Bascomb suggested that Wells' grave remarks had been better leveled at the radical Republicans, whose mulatto adherents he charged with practicing voodoo. "The secret associations, that all here seated are best advised to smoke out and trample, are the clubs of the snake, of the black cat, and the plumed cock; for their guiding tenet is one and the same with that of our opponents in this very body: unholy union, the mixing of the bloods."

Jessamine Marie DuClous Bascomb

The city is cleaner now. The ever recurring tides of mud are no more. Yet the fine dust in the air remains. Perhaps this late arrival of hygienics is a great irony. Or perhaps not. I do not presume to know anything more than what I see, these days. But I suppose the trend started when Spoons Butler did it for the first time ever, mandated that the streets be cleaned, at the point of a bayonet in '63. Or when? My memory has become as trackless as Barataria. Such is the price of never forgetting.

Whither the yellow and red turbaned *marchandes*, their great baskets brimming over with flowers, under the broad arcades of the *rue Royale?* The flapping canvas awnings and cracked red tile roofs, do these remain? I had a father, a mother, a roan horse. Lovers. We were once hemmed in all around by a slithering, watery wilderness, all draped in foliage and fumes. But now the black water is gone, from river to lake; the thick and teeming verdure, I am sure, has been cut back, and everything paved over. This, too, was the fate of the mud, which once lapped at the stoops of our very houses.

In waking I busy myself with the problems of a new girl. In point of fact, she is the cause which brings me before you now—if indeed you are there. To distinguish among shade, phantom of memory, and living man is no light task for us. The new girl is most certainly one of our number, however. This much I know, though she knows it not yet. I am not sure what her years numbered when she arrived on our listless shores, but, in that she had the time to learn love of man and quite a bit about boudoir matters, she must already have been a young woman. The difficulty is that she has brought with her some unwholesome burden from her past which threatens our very existence, a thing we cherish as much as flesh and blood do theirs, as do also the lowliest insects, as do fish, even. Her attachment to her recent life normally would be no cause for surprise or alarm, but for the man she remembers. This man, who was the new girl's sometime lover, must remember something of her as well, for he now vainly seeks her, even while he claims a different and more grandiose purpose for meddling with the bands that so fitly separate us. In that lustful self-aggrandizement is his principal aim in life, he is not unlike the leading men of my day. Warmoth. Banks. Bascomb, my father. Yet this young unbuttered man has no entourage, probably because he lacks even the refinement of a low sort like my father. And whatever insults the tyrants of my time may have perpetrated on their unwilling subjects, one always assumed that death would entail escape from the folly, degradation, and violence that was their coin.

Because Mills Loomis Mills, so lacking in stature among living men, casts his net about in our realm instead, I, too, feel called upon to tug at the threads of the curtain between us, between us and them, us and you all. To somehow learn of and prevent the great calamity that Mills Loomis Mills would bring down upon us, I am driven out into hours of the brightest sunlight, to seek him out and observe him.

There he rides now, on a steamer, a strange steamer, for its stacks emit no smoke. Yet miraculously, the boat churns forward. No soot rains down on the heads of them who crowd the upper decks. Mills Loomis Mills creeps there among the unsuspecting others. Plying the rivers not in search of vistas or an easy fortune, but in search of us, with the intent to harm us. Yet I remain sure that he, like so many comparable temperaments before him, "knows not what he does."

While the others make the trip for diversion's sake, this Mills hopes that his special detective powers will find some vindication in the unmapped swamps of Barataria, that he will sense some phenomenon there in the unpeopled wilderness that the teeming city would unlikely allow.

Soul resin? If I had not long ago despaired of prayer, I would ardently bend my knees to stop him, knowing not of any more promising course of action. This soul resin could be the annihilation of us all.

The new girl is lovely, though, in appearance as well as spirit. The most luxuriant red curls. A fine, full red mouth. And she has such a brightness about her. Her brilliance touches us all who are close to her with warmth and the most unexpected sense of stillness and contentment. Also—and in this she is more fortunate than I— the fragrance about her is a delight. It smells like some nice woods somewhere, of pine? Like the forests around St. Francisville? Or Natchez? We knew some people up there. On a piney slope some evening-time before the volcanic events of my day scattered my family and my thoughts, my father, possessing both his legs, chased me up and down wearing a great pumpkin on his head. Leaves were burning. The air was blue and crisp. He conjured up strange growling sounds and hunkered over like some fancied beast. Then our play was over and he reclined against a stump—there were many stumps—I on his lap, small, and he said out here in the woods is where men and women were truly made, but that the day was coming when people would be more and more city-made, that it would mean a dire and terrible disbalance for society, that it would mean ruin. I asked him why, then, did we live in the city? For we did. We lived in the city and I cannot recall why we were often elsewhere. Family? Flight from fever? I do recall his reply: he said we were in the city only long enough for him to secure us a fit place in the countryside, that it would not do for me, a little lady, to live in the rugged circumstances that he the boy had known. He added, "And your mother!" and this caused him so great amusement that he laughed until violent coughing seized him, and he pushed me from his lap and stood until it passed.

I am not sure how she is called yet, but the new girl smells like spicy rich pine sap, like the marrow of young, surging, living trees; so until I learn her given name I will call her my sylph. I am looking forward to knowing her, and my only regret is my impatience that it will take so long—one never knows—to be able to converse with her. My apprehension concerning her is that she is too blissful: I fear she may be so fresh that she has not yet caught up with the circumstances of her death. There are bruises, marks on her which suggest she may have passed not from ailment or birthing, but by some spiteful human hand.

Mills Loomis Mills

The Mississippi Belle is a slap in the face to anybody that loves truth. That's why it's a poetic irony that it's showing me what I need to be shown to do my thing and change the world. Those red drinks aren't bad, though. And the breeze is nice, and for some reason the calliope seemed fine to me, too, even though I know it's supposed to be tacky. It gives the whole river ride a breezy carnival type feel, makes it clear from the start that the whole trip is about Disney, not real. Those gray warboats with their guns in the Navy yard, they're not real, the docked tankers and fireboats with hoses, and the smoking towers of the petrochem factories. The half-swamped leaning towers of trees on the wrong side of the levee—all an exhibit stamped safe for family entertainment. But how can they look down at the river, into the backstabbing eddies and dead-end express currents without just a little bit of old-fashioned awe and downright fear for that thing that would kick their ass if given half a chance, the Mississippi? The hooting calliope and the red drinks with orange and pineapple and cherry garnish, and the dumb ruffled pink shirts and pseudo-red vest things on the waiters, they're all designed to help the happy Florida families buy into the Big Lie—that they're safe.

So the whole enterprise is disgusting but somehow bittersweetly fun too, like if you catch an episode of *Speed Racer* or *Johnny Quest* years after childhood and realize with a sneer and a smile that the animation's pitifully cheap. So you enjoy it with one half of yourself, but with the other half it's time to turn the tube off and track the truth, the one truth, the resin. The TV and the tourist-boat and booze and everything, it all comes tumbling down after you get your first whiff of old soul. At first it smelled to me like manure, but then it smelled like incredible amounts of different things in rapid succession, which makes sense if you think about it.

I don't want to give the blindly stabbing Mississippi Belle too much credit, though. It's just fate, like most things are (sorry, Marx!), that its tourist bayou route crosses pretty close by a site that I learned about from my researches. A *possible* site, that is. That's all reading print or even talking to people will get you—possibilities. That's where the classroom stops, too. The rest of the wild blue yonder is all nose and ears.

And after nose and ears comes nerve. The toil under the sun I've already done. Research. What Ecclesiastes says our life is. Toil. Plus my stuff on the side to get ready. Training. Sneaking. Snooping around where people don't want me because they're too small to have vision, people like the police and the liberal academic types. A brand new century and nobody's figured out how to tap our country's most vital resource, and there it is, as plain as flying shit in the face of every tourist and lackey and hack that suckers it on the Mississippi Belle. Yet it's me or nobody. So it's me. I'm gonna use it. The power. The soul resin. The stuff is fuel.

Rafe Vidrine

I suppose I should understand something about Mills' irrational behavior. I've lost a wife, only a year ago. Of course the nature of the two women's deaths is in no way similar. Lauren's was drawn out, breast cancer. It was routinely, almost blandly devastating. Mills' girlfriend, April Brunnen, was murdered. Far away, in New Mexico. I wonder how he was notified. At least he didn't have to witness it.

Mattie LaVonne has taught me an old Indian trick. Directed dreaming. The purpose is to seek out that relic of Lauren remaining in my psyche and to spend time with her in my dreams. I have the strangest sense that Mills is mucking it up somehow. I go looking for Lauren and find someone else. It's not Mills, though, so my suspicions are probably more evidence of old-age paranoia than anything else. It's a she, she's been inserting herself in the space where Lauren should be. Some astray image, I guess from my deep memory, of a woman whose acquaintance I don't recall. At first some mechanism in myself suppressed the memory of these dreams immediately upon waking. I would remember seeing Lauren—in progressively more worn, stale reproductions—and then someone else, vaguely. Not even an image, rather a sense of a presence. Lately whenever I wake from these excursions my first sensation is a palpable smell of vomit. I wake up smelling it and immediately check myself to see if I've thrown up during the night. But the vomit's never there, not even the taste of it in my throat. Just the smell. When I try to remember past the smell, Lauren's image crops up all too dutifully, then fades fast—I may have been superimposing it during the waking process. There's always a deeper layer of image, though. Stiff figures. As in a wax museum. Apparently speaking. People I've read and written about. One alone moves among them. A woman. Not my wife.

Dear Mills,

I miss miss miss miss miss you! I know my last letter probably bummed you out but I feel much better now. I've made some OK friends and New Mexico's really starting to grow on me. Remember how I said it was unnatural for people to live in a place with so little water? But I'm really starting to dig it now. I guess when you're in a new place you have to look for what's unique and cool about that place and stop looking for stuff from the place you used to be in. I'm looking forward to coming back home, but it's like I don't even want to think about it 'cause it's a couple of months off still.

But hey guess what? I think my mom's gonna give me my best birthday present ever: A plane ticket for you to come visit me! Then I would really love it here. Could you figure out a way to smuggle 'Shoba? Then everything would be perfect.

OK, love-boy, I have to go because I have to pack to go camping up in the Sangre de Cristos-beautiful mountains, I can't believe I didn't notice them when I first got here. It's because I couldn't get you

49

out of my mind, you cad! Smoke a joint on the levee for me and throw the roach in the river. I'll drop a roach for you in the Pecos Gulch, where I'm going.

A-
XOXOXOX

Mills Loomis Mills

Like oil, it's a fossil fuel. The first step is, some human soul dies by bleeding, preferably slowly. The state of mind of the dying bleeder has got to be bitter. My contact told me the bleeder has to curse God in the final moments. Whatever they do, though, it does something to the blood, prepares it, and also chains the soul in place and time. Unlike the other dead, it can't move and it can't remember. But check this: the blood must not be cleaned up or molested in any way by human hand. This allows the *blood cycle* to take root and develop. After some term (at least fifty years) of the blood soaking into the land, being evaporated by the sun, and rained back onto the land, the blood cycle is over, and a residue remains. This residue—soul resin—can survive anywhere from fifty years to several centuries. They may just be around forever—not like you'd want to be it, though. No way.

So who am I, and how and when did I decide that I was going to be more important than Einstein and Washington and Lincoln and everybody else besides Jesus and the Buddha? Well, Jesus—he knew about blood didn't he? If he didn't know, he sure found out. And the Buddha, he would say, "It's not me, man, it's what I'm doing," so that's what I say. But I did get the call, as opposed to somebody else getting it. NO, I didn't kill anybody! But I knew somebody that got killed, somebody close to me, well, a "loved one" I guess you'd say. But, scientists agree, whatever "relationship" I may have had with that person is not important because what's key is that the blood emitted a sound (first time I heard it) which I then began to look hard into.

She didn't likely become soul resin, anyway, because it really doesn't happen too often. Because of the demands of the blood cycle, the site where the soul resin is at has to be a place where sky, land, and water exist together on the same plane—i.e. around sea-level. And since land is an intrusion dividing water and sky like day divides night, the trick is to keep the land variable at a minimum. Blood has closer ties with water than with land, it needs humidity to mature—but obviously it must fall on land or else it just gets all diluted and dispersed till it's barely blood anymore.

But it wasn't geography that landed me in the Crescent City, it was culture. An unusually high number of the kind of deaths that make the dying lift their voices in an unholy bitch-fit against God (basically something like "hey, fuck you, God"—people do it). Such an act damns the blood to eternal hell on Earth, the repetition of those last bad moments (because these are bad-type deaths, where people get mad) throughout eternity.

(Take my advice, keep your cool when you go. The Man upstairs is *vengeful*.)

But I couldn't hope to find the stuff actually in New Orleans, either. The problem with cities is that, even though more people are murdered and killed in accidents, bodies are usually discovered and blood is usually cleaned up. Sure, there's a great deal of fresh blood in cities, but fresh blood is worthless. The blood must rest undisturbed at the spot where it was shed. For fifty years, at least. Or else no blood cycle, no soul resin, no cigar.

Right, but cities are great for developing skills. That's why I've spent the past eight months earning my freak reputation, reading police reports and visiting the scenes of high blood-loss crimes. Knifings, gut shots, bludgeonings—they flayed this one guy! Man, was that loud. Like fifteen-hundred kindergarten classes scratching their fingernails across blackboards. Anyway, I had to get used to the sound. Of course, freshly spilled blood has a much different sound than the blood of soul resin age. Fresh blood has a high-pitched, bell-like ring. Like desperate screeching or squeaking at barely audible volumes. Lots of people hear this sound every day but don't know what it is.

That squeaky whining of the fresh stuff was the only blood-sound I knew before I hauled my ass onto that riverboat and took a ride out where people don't go much by land. But now I know: the sound of the mature soul resin blood is much more of a true moan, a charcoal-mellowed stentorian whisper. It sounds like moving air, like the rumbling sigh of trucks on a highway you didn't realize was there, until you heard it. A sound that's rarely to be glimpsed in today's cities. You really have to get away from the noise of a city to where a body can bleed freely and escape detection for a while. Like go on a fishing or a hunting trip and see what you can turn up. Or even a bayou cruise. Hey, I'm living proof. I started to smell it around 12:15, about five miles downriver from Petit Bois. The ex-guy I'm gonna meet. His remains, I mean. A historical figure that everybody including the almighty Rafe Vidrine thought was pretty humble and didn't amount to much, shit-ass victim number eight-million-and-three, who finally gets his glory half a century after his forgotten death.

53

May 30, 1942

The body of a Negro youth that was discovered on Tuesday in the neighborhood of Barataria Bay, near the mouth of the Tchefuncte River, has been identified as seventeen-year old Lucius Holt, Jr. of Petit Bois. The editor wishes to extend condolences, on the behalf of the entire community, to the Holt family, who have always been fine people. His grandfather, the proprietor of the Get a'Holt Grocery and Cafe in Petit Bois, has closed his business for the time-being "to grieve and reflect." He regrets that his son, Lucius Holt, Sr., cannot be with the family at this difficult time, for he is currently doing his part with our sailors in the Pacific.

Memorial services will be held tomorrow at the China Grove M.B. Church at 956 Myrtle St. in Petit Bois on Saturday.

Jessamine Marie DuClous Bascomb

His face is like his ambition. He is neither bearded nor beardless. The hairs upon his head are similarly of divided mind: some lie flat against his skull, refusing to budge even in the vigorous delta breezes, while other contingents stretch longingly skyward and twitter there. He wears a well-soiled combed-cotton shirt of some lighter shade, though it is impossible to determine which. He sports also, and I don't know whether in defiance of season or not, a great black topcoat many sizes too large for his slight frame. His eyes are deep brown and un-readable, nothing like the magnanimous brown of the river he now looks out upon. In fact, his entire face betrays not a hint of the roaring furnace of rage and ambition it masks. Do not ask how I presume to know so much about the heated private loomings of Mills Loomis Mills. I know the type, that is what matters. He has learned enough about a thing to perceive an interest in it for himself, he cares not to read on and hear of consequences.

I cannot possibly discern which feature of body or spirit once so forcefully drew my sylph to him, such that even in her current state she will not forget.

But of course this is not true. I understand all too well, having similarly erred and paid the ultimate price. Politics is a male art. They play it ruthlessly, as they do their war games, as they do their *contre-temps* with the women who attempt to love them. It is the way he now so resolutely grasps the banister and peers out over the treetops receding, so full of purpose that no energy is left for laughing or smiling, for conversing with his companions, unless, of course, it be a useful stratagem. My sylph must have fallen prey to her sense that his will was solidly bolted to his person, unflaggable. And now also it is the way he turns from the view, from his purpose, as if sure in his knowledge that what he seeks is already easily within his reach, that he may then lightly postpone it, that he may pass the time looking with his quiet and sinister visage on the unsuspecting pleasure-seekers surrounding him. Now finally he does smile, but no mortal fellow shares it, it rises out of his extravagant solitary pride: it is an expression of disdain for them who share the boat with him. He has presumed them all guilty, therefore expendable. And this judgment extends even to me, I know it already, and I have not yet even shared his bed though I know that I will regardless of my knowledge of his character. Is it the squareness of his shoulders, his upright chin and immaculate erect carriage that causes me so to forget myself? This man whom my father would like to have murdered, this un-white—though golden—body in its exorbitant finery of Paris, Brussels. The glinting ruby in his cravat. Alphonse. Narcisse, as his sister taught me to call him. Your warbling French, quoting verse of Chateaubriand or Lanusse in a voice like my mother's, singing Berlioz, *Les nuits d'été*. Or your English, declaiming in the tone of the *New Orleans Tribune*. Yes, the voice is what seduced me, so like the river bearing us both into the coming night, soft to the touch yet unshakable in its destination. Or simply this: that I know the destination he has set his irrepressible energies to, it is to me, and perhaps this is enough. But he, like my father, is also a politician and no more to be trusted. Why would I give myself to such a sort? On the other hand, why should I not and who is to keep me from it?

It appears the riverboats used to ferry about more noble men. I make no claim to follow anymore the vagaries of fashion, but not even the dress of Mills Loomis Mills seems suitable for society. He is a species of demagogue, I suppose. Not "one of us," to use my father's phrase. There, how he strikes up conversation with a deckhand, wishing to incite something, hailing him "brother" when the two surely have never met. "So how long you been working with this outfit?"

"Year."

"Ever notice any weird smells out on the bayous?"

"What are you, a fed or something?"

By "fed" he means a "federal"? New Orleans again under occupation? Have the cowards retraced the steps of their flight?

"No," he laughs, or pretends it well, "Tourist. Well, private citizen. Just doing my own research."

"And you wanna know do I smell anything out here? Well you oughta open up your nose. It stinks. Sewage. Chemicals. They call this whole stretch of river the cancer corridor."

I should have known. The city is not cleaner, it merely appears so.

"Yeah, I know. High incidence of cancer, yeah. Heart disease too, buddy. But don't worry about my nose. It's a gastronomist of the beyond."

"What?"

"Yeah. But I'm talking about something you can't identify that easy, it's not like a smell you could name, it's something you've never smelled before."

"How would I be able to tell you I smelled it then?" The deckhand, leaning on some kind of electrically powered broom-like contraption, has clearly decided that Mills is no more than an amusing and harmless half-wit. Loomis Mills must often benefit from this, from being underestimated by his opponents and fellows alike.

"Have you heard anything, then? Like a high-pitched squeaking, or, even better, a really low rumbling? Out somewhere where you thought nothing was?"

The deckhand pauses, reflects, and nods assent. His grin has contracted somewhat, though not completely. "Yes."

"Know what it is?"

"No."

He speaks of soul resin. He steers ever closer on his black tide.

Is this why you are here, child, to warn and thus ward off the madness your former lover intends? Or are you rather a confederate in his design? When will you ever speak? If I could induce you through punishments, I would.

Though, of course, you need not fear me for I have no hand to strike with. Ah, my poor *sylphide,* such a wealth of pictures, sensations, and snippets of stories you are, yet so untenanted. The accumulations of your short life spill out from you as if no one is at home, as if there is no housekeeper to tidy it all. Such like is *terre à terre*, and I should not let it disturb me so, were it not for the urgency of the times we find ourselves in. From our end alone I cannot influence the goings-on of the outer world, no matter how threatening to us or barbarous such activities may be. So exhausting. There are other pastimes to while away an eternity with. Memory, for example. Such as the memory of him who was hanged, this Clouet. The golden man with black enough ambition to storm my bed, and heart, only finally to die on the field of vainglory. I did not witness the solemnities, though I warrant I can picture it well. The principle players, the unrepentant high-chinned stare of the condemned man, the gruff decorum of his sentencers. I picture it in the square before the Mechanic's Institute, though it was most likely not a public event. Most likely it took place under a dreary rain in the courtyard of the parish prison.

When I was young, just old enough to command my own carriage, I was used to making excursions to that neighborhood. I had first, of course, always to evade my *milatraisse*, my mother's spy. I believe the first time was at my driver's suggestion, for I had complained from want of distraction, and he always seemed to know the answer to my whims. Through the glass of my coupe or from the open air of my cabriolet, I would survey the faces of the men and women filing from omnibus to jail. They were a varied assortment. Every morning met by jeering street children, who often threw stones. This was a great entertainment for me, to see the range of human feeling there displayed; the seasoned ruffian with the brazen grin, or the new initiate, often in fine but overworn linen, shedding ill-hid tears of shame or fear.

I have never learned how he comported himself on his way to the scaffold, but I do believe I have seen him since, though it be long ago and but a fleeting glance through a thousand other faces. The once beloved face I could not make out at all, for his head was draped in ceremonial black cloth.

My exasperation in this matter has caused me to break from tradition and reach out to you, and for that I beg your forgiveness. However, I am in a position to reciprocate your kindness. One day you will need me fully as much as I need you now, and rare is the guide hired before this journey.

We are not sure where Mills Loomis Mills plans to make his incursion, but practicality suggests that he make it in the region around New Orleans. He has found soul resin somewhere, and he intends, for the sake of some feverish design, to activate the resin and thus convert it to energy, exactly as one might burn fuel. The great danger lies in a technical flaw of which he is not aware. His error is that he greatly overestimates the separateness of soul resin from the rest of us. We are not all in our own little spaces over here. Once uncontained, the black pitch of the soul resin may absorb many more souls than the number who rightfully deserve it. I have told you much of Mills Loomis Mills in our previous correspondences. Of his interest in the life of blood after it spills. Of his morbid fascination with those unfortunates who become soul resin. If he succeeds, how many of us may be sucked into his puncture of the fragile membrane of Perdition? Recall that you, too, have a loved one who is now among our ranks.

It was wise of you to notify the police. It would be beneficial to our interest if the police should detain him. As long as he remains in the city, we may rest. There is not likely any soul resin in the city.

Dear Mills,

I'm taking your advice and remembering all the good times I've had. You said I should remember the three best times in my life, and they were all with you. But you said it would make me feel better about being where I'm at, and I can't figure out why you say that. If all my best times were with you, how could it be good when I'm not with you? I know "distance makes the heart grow fonder."

OK, here's my three best times:

1. The third time we fucked. Remember? It was the first time I got off (with a guy). It's 'cause you were really drunk so you took a long time and I was totally straight so it was easy. We were on the levee and it was slanted so we kept sliding but it was OK. And the joggers kept running by and they didn't look down and notice us. And we didn't notice till after, but there was the red ant pile that our feet were in, and then I noticed all these red bumps and noticed how it hurt. You said later how the best part wasn't the sex, but feeling the ant bites get itchy later and how it would remind us of the sex, but only as long as they still itched. I thought that was a really cool thing to say. It's so you.

2. We get 'Shoba. The best part was on the drive back from Mississippi and there was that cool kid in the rest stop who told us he was visiting his dad in the penitentiary and we bought him a Mountain Dew (yahoo!). And then when we ate the fried chicken and little 'Shoba was all curled up and sleeping in the little shoebox and it was that really heavy sunset. Remember? I cried and you wanted to know why and I said I didn't know? I still don't know.

3. Our home. Actually this is Number One. Put the other ones after this. Just us at home together. Skipping class or whatever. You making the coffee while I make the eggs 'n beans. Our naps.

I miss you. But like you said, our reunion will be our funnest day together ever. 'Til then, I know a way we can stay in touch really—that thing in the package is a "dream catcher." You're supposed to hang it over your bed. That stone I tied to the feathers is pretty rare—a guy at a rock shop told me it was "igneous quartzite." I found it out in the desert and I've been wearing it in my token-bag and sleeping with it all week, so now I'll be with you when we're both sleeping!

In love and lust,
April

P.S. I really <u>really</u> like this Johnny Cash disc you sent me and I know it's supposed to make me into being out here but it just kind of creeps me out for some reason. So I'm sending it back so you can dig it and think about me out here. Send me some Nevilles or something to remind me of home?

A

Mills Loomis Mills

I saw in a movie or read in a book once where this holy man got the call but somebody said, "Are you sure?" and he said, "Am I sure what?"

"Are you sure it was the Lord calling you?"

"Well, who else would it be?"

"You know."

It went like that and that's something I have to sorta wonder about, myself. You see somebody had to tell me all this stuff, about the soul resin and how to pick it up out of the general racket. That somebody, moreover, would have to be a dead somebody. And can you trust them?

It was a guy I think. But he sounded gay, so I'm not sure. He was pretty secretive about himself. You know what? I don't think he had a head. I don't see how that's possible, since I don't see how he could talk (or whatever they do) without one, but the way I remember it, the dude had no head. Maybe he kept it with him in a bag or something? As far as why I couldn't see him too well, that could be because he couldn't project himself much because he was weak or because he was recently dead—which I doubt—or it could be that he wanted it that way.

To see or hear the dead at all you have to go to this space inside yourself and look out from there—at least that's what I do. I guess some people—crazy people—have no control over it, there's just dead people crawling all over them all the time (and people wonder why they freak out). It comes and goes for me, too. I can't always do it. But I remember the first night. I mean, I'd had strange dreams before, and that should have clued me in, but I remember the night I first actually heard the blood and felt it. It was the night April died, maybe she was trying to reach me and it didn't exactly work. She was far away, so something else happened—this mess.

I was actually studying that night. I was trying to get my shit together. Had all these plans, more like fantasies, of me and April being studious student types, in a little room we were going to make into a study with matching desks, her with her glasses, us looking up from books to share tidbits.

She was coming back in two days. I had just dragged up this table somebody left by the sidewalk that I thought she might want for her desk. There was a mellow rain—like a fall rain, not a summer storm—and 'Shoba was curled up on the couch next to me, and I had April's picture on the coffee table and one of her letters, where I could look up from my book and see them when I wanted. I was reading Vidrine's book, <u>Beyond Yellow and Black: Franco-African Political Culture in Louisiana.</u>

Then me and 'Shoba went to bed. It was the last time I felt something like normal, peaceful, in my life. The drizzling rain meant fall which meant coolness and April coming back. 'Shoba was dog-snoring next to me, and I had this scarf of April's that I slept with that summer, a yellow paisley '60s thing, it would be around her neck, sometimes with sundresses and sometimes with cut-offs and a t-shirt. I had it next to my head on the pillow for going to sleep.

I woke up from 'Shoba growling. It happened whenever somebody he didn't know walked too close by our window. But he wasn't looking at the window. April's paisley scarf was acting weird, twitching and stretching apparently all on its own. Then at the same time 'Shoba let loose barking, wild, his hair all up-ended like a cat's, and the scarf made a sound, too, like a table-saw just got turned on suddenly in the next room at the highest setting and started cutting through a two-by-four, a long one, lengthways. Needless to say, I was from that moment on freaked for life. Already, even if that was it and nothing else happened, I would've been a waste for anything except the most crazy proposition. Then the scarf started giving off a glow like candlelight, and it seemed like some haze passed through it, like on a hot day the road ahead of you blurs in a haze, that's what seemed to actually be coming out of the scarf. And like when you light a candle, how the edges of a room get darker and you can't see them anymore, a liquidy darkness draped the walls and then everything everywhere except right around me and the scarf. 'Shoba had quit barking and now he was whining high and trying to claw the window open enough to get out. And the haze coming out of the scarf like different density air, some of the molecules of it got together enough to be something like a hand touching my face.

Then the scarf stopped doing its thing, but still the room was different. It always would be. Everything was different forever after that moment. I knew then that some weird person-like thing was around. It was the guy, the guy who was all set to spill everything about soul resin but had to wait awhile for me to be able to handle it. I knew already that some bad thing had happened to

April. But the first thing the guy's voice said was, "She is gone out of the land of the living, yet you may still one day look upon her."

Rafe Vidrine

About two weeks after the police contacted me, I began to resent my involvement in the whole Mills Loomis Mills business. In our telephone interview of October 8, the detective had refused to say what the case was about. This didn't bother me until I reflected and became aware that in fact I knew very much about the case, but could not remember how I had come to learn it. I knew: a) that the boy had not actually broken the law, b) that the police had come to think of him as a nuisance, but not a danger to society, c) that Mills Loomis Mills had developed a theoretical technology that was for some reason considered dangerous by someone, and d) that my knowledge of these things had been transmitted incrementally and without my cognition. The trite thing to add was never more appropriate—"sounds crazy, I know"—and that's why I haven't told any one.

On November 2 I decided to visit the First Precinct and fabricate some pretense that might help me get some explanations. I had difficulty finding it because the station house had recently been moved. It didn't surprise me to learn of its new location, in what had been the Quarter's tourist welcome center. A simple columned neo-classical cube, plain, even sparse. Built before the drunkenness of King Cotton and King Cane took over. Before the tacky American excesses. I knew it had started out as a thriving slave exchange, but I was surprised that this fact was not omitted from the plaque on the gate. I saw no evidence of its original mission inside, though it did maintain the character of a tourism bureau, which made the uniformed officers look somewhat surreal lounging around in front of computer screens in the pseudo-antebellum decor.

The detective who had originally interviewed me was allegedly unavailable, so I stated the lie I came to state: that I had received a threatening phone call from Mills Loomis Mills. The ploy worked. I won an audience with an annoyed underling who tried to look concerned.

"When did you receive the phone call?"

"Last night, during the night."

"What time exactly, sir?"

"I don't recall."

"What did he say?"

I hadn't bothered to develop my lie and prepare it for public use. I had no idea what Mills was supposed to have said. But I surprised myself with the depth of plausible detail I was able to apply. I said that the boy had mentioned blood, that he'd heard the rumbling of blood and that it spoke to him of new scientific directions. That he had learned how to tap the energy of departed souls, but that the one obstacle remaining was the need to delineate between fresh and old blood. Then I lent urgency to the tale by saying that the phone-call (the lie) caused me to fear for my life.

The officer said, "Yeah, that's him all right," and added that Mills Loomis Mills had been turning up at homicide investigations over the past few months.

"How did he find out about them?"

"Police report in the paper, I guess."

"How detailed are these reports?"

But all I got after that were sealed lips and stubborn grinning head-shaking. I said, "I'm not the press," without believing it, but it failed to make him trust me. He offered to have my phone tapped, but I was repelled by the idea and let him know it. He said he'd get back to me. In New Orleans that means goodbye.

I went home and dutifully tried to feel some remorse at wrongfully incriminating someone. But instead of remorse I felt my previous anxiety giving way to a more productive anger, because the boy *was* up to something and had somehow dragged me, a man who thought he deserved repose after all these years, into some piece of insanity. But how had he done it?

Trouble always comes at the wrong time, of course, but I did have a deadline to meet. Mattie LaVonne was putting together a new journal—*Osceola*—with a focus on early efforts at common cause among people of color, particularly between Native American and black. I had promised Mattie an article for the premier issue on Alphonse Clouet, the outspoken mulatto entrepreneur and politico whose radical shift in racial thinking during Reconstruction—from *gens de couleur* solidarity to a more American, color-based separatism—bought him such unlikely allies in and beyond New Orleans. Then he was charged with poisoning a white woman who was alleged to have been his mistress. A fascinating case which I had been enjoying immensely.

So is Mills Loomis Mills, of course, a fascinating case. But I'll admit it, I'd much rather immerse myself in morbidness which is past and does not affect me directly. This is not a historian's weakness, it's a human one.

On the afternoon of November 2, I hoped to put Mills out of my mind and get some work done. So I turned on my computer, opened a book, made coffee, and realized that Mills alone couldn't shoulder all the blame for my restlessness, which made me feel better. Because the coffee distracted me, too. Because of Lauren. I threw in a dash of vanilla because that's how she used to drink it. Before I read or wrote a word, I sat and tried to touch in my memory the smell of Lauren in fresh linen on the back porch, mingled with our honeysuckles. Then just the taste of tobacco smoke, another lost love.

Then I dozed off and the real dreaming began. Since about June my regular dream-cycle had begun to have an added dimension, a shift. Sooner or later I began to suspect that Mills had a hand in it, some kind of dream manipulation. Yes, I'm becoming superstitious. I'm not willing to lapse into churchgoing yet, though. I'm as doubtful and healthily skeptical of my superstitions as anyone could expect. I'm only writing this down now because the pattern has become so obvious that it's assumed a rationality of its own. It has, in effect, proven itself. At some point in every dream, if I stay in it long enough, comes an invisible screen through which everything changes. Like a change in lighting—like a cloud suddenly passing over or moving away. The frames of my dreams have continued to be occupied by people, places, and events that I believe belong to my own memory. Lauren is almost always there. Mattie taught me how to invoke her. Of course I know that it's not really her but only a fading picture of her called up from some failing place in my mind. The point always comes, though, when the flat image and aura of Lauren blinks into an animated presence that looks so much like her, but who, and I'm absolutely sure of this by now, is a woman I have never met before. On the afternoon of November 2 she was there again, like clockwork, but I was in no mood for it. I wanted either to work or really rest, and I was beginning to resent that I was no longer allowed to do either.

After I woke myself up I heard the coffee cup hitting the floor and rolling. Rolling? Now that I write this it doesn't seem possible, but that's what I heard. What I saw in front of me was the face still. Like Lauren's, but with jet hair pulled back and a black-ribboned cameo choker on an ivory neck. The color scheme resembled piano keys. I reached my hand out to touch her but remembered that a) whoever it was wasn't Lauren, and b) whoever it was wasn't really there.

Again, a lingering odor of acidic bile remained. I got up out of the chair and gargled, and dumped out the pot of coffee and stuck a Trident in my mouth and chewed it. I picked up my Alphonse Clouet manuscript and put it down.

Then the name came to me: Lucius Holt. The last time I spoke with Mills he had still been raving about his plans to uncover some earth-shattering new revelation about the Holt incident. Then I heard a voice stating the name. *Lucius Holt.* It was memory, but it was recent and I didn't know how that could be possible. A woman's voice. Not Lauren, not Mattie LaVonne. My uninvited dream-guest? The brain works in strange ways. So then I resolved to get off my backside and actually use that brain in a way I was more familiar with. Get down to a fluorescent lighted room to see if the paper trail to Lucius Holt might lead me to the live footsteps of Mills Loomis Mills. But I couldn't help but worry that some deterioration was afoot in my mind. Maybe the smell of vomit was the smell of my own decaying brain-cells. But the woman? Gray-eyed in an elaborate black longsleeved dress, shouting, face contorted, but all that comes out is a raspy indecipherable whisper.

Jessamine Marie DuClous Bascomb

I know, Mr. Vidrine, that the press of so many voiceless faces and faceless voices leaves you turned round and round, as in "blind man's buff". But we need each other now as neither of us has needed another before. We have a common adversity in Mills Loomis Mills, whom I think you know? Because of his impatience and incomplete learning, he now poses a dire threat. Now he is one who, having learned to knead the dough, still believes that the bread will rise without yeast. He must know two things, and these you must apprise him of. There is one dear to him, the only one he knows who has died, I presume it is his love for her that drives his blunder into such a reckless pass. His reluctance to admit it I attribute to you all's ill-conceived god Science, your god of short-cuts, whose very name stings the ears of the true God, who, were it not for His own pride, would beg Mills to abandon this devilment he has taken upon himself.

The second thing I implore you to hear—can you?— is that she, Mills' beloved, is not only she. He has an inkling into these matters, I know, for he has found us, after all, even if the we he has found are too many conveniently to be processed and refined.

I do not know her name. She is yet too new here to assert herself with effect. You—Vidrine, Loomis, whoever may hear me—you know that the mass of all of us is so overpowering, can't you then reason that if any voice, any face, presents itself to you, that it must needs be the result of a volition from our end of things? She is here with me, Mills, only mute, as she possibly will be for the rest of your time in the day. I give you this warning: if you attempt to use any of us as some extractive resource, like Alabama anthracite or Menominee iron, you abuse only her, the one you pretend not to love and fail to see, though her red curls glow so brightly.

Mills Loomis Mills

The Mississippi Belle showed me, took me there (near enough almost to touch, but not quite) and the tourists, pre-occupied with the film in their cameras (mine was empty, a prop), proved as clueless as their ancestors. The nautical junkyard at the mouth of the Tchefuncte, it's a garden. Old tugboats, barges, trawlers, laid to rest after decades of loyal service. It's a graveyard with invisible flowers. Flowers like Catalpa, sweet fragrance on a foundation of crotch stink.

Why would I care about a dirty slough full of trashed boats? Because more than boats had been laid to rest there. A person had expired there, too, about fifty, seventy-five years ago. That person bled and bled. More than enough blood. I heard the yawn of ripe soul resin more loud and clear than any textbook scenario could ever even hint at. It reached out to me like God never reached out to Adam.

The best way to judge the quality of soul resin is to measure the sharpness of the blood's life memories. That's why I knew I was in business. Because the blood of whoever died on the Tchefuncte had a lot to show me.

Of course, most of what I saw in the blood was useless for my purposes. If I were a detective, like the pussies at NOPD and their social workers try to be, I'd care about cause of death, perpetrator, blah blah blah. That kind of thing doesn't really concern me. But sometimes there are fun tid-bits. The content of the victim's mind immediately before and at the point of death is flashed over and over again like a thirty-second tape loop. It can get pretty tedious sometimes, but that's the price of fruitful research.

In this case: sometime before his/her death, the future bleeder passed by an open window (in a humble wooden residential structure with a low and rusty tin roof) and witnessed sexual activity between a man and a woman. I lingered and watched. The man's back was facing the window, but the woman's face was in full view above the man's shoulder. They were awkwardly twisted up in a faded green sheet. A radio was on. The voice on the radio talked about aircraft carriers and Nimitz and Tojo. It was a balmy afternoon—felt like April or November, but mid-May is most likely (1941, *Battle of the Coral Sea*). The taste of sweat, and flat and warm grape soda was in my mouth. The woman opened her eyes and saw me through the window. She stared at me for whole seconds. At first her look was about thrill, secret complicity, mmmm. Then the open mouth begging to have an organ in it became the open mouth of shock, pissed-offness. She screamed and pushed the guy off her. She'd sighted me. But I knew who I was before she did.

Lucius Holt.

Of course, this incident may or may not have something to do with the eventual death. Depends on the personality of the departed. Something we can never hope to know.

The other information stored in the blood was much more fragmentary. People I don't know doing

78

normal things. Contrary to the impression you get from the movies, people did normal things fifty-three years ago just like we do them today.

So at least one tourist didn't feel jilted for shelling out the thirty bucks for the Mississippi Belle's pollution tour. The other tourists got more for their money than they usually do, too, because I did a rash and stupid thing because I was so caught up in the stretching yawning creepers of sound and smell old Lucius was sending out to me. I took off my raincoat and my shoes. The people looked. I got up on the railing. A guy made a dash for me. I wanted to dive down off of three stories of riverboat into the loving crotch of death river. For mankind. They need it.

But the clueless assholes would have dragged me back out, anyway. So I just got down before the lug rushing at me got a chance to knock the whole railing over. I laughed and said, "Hey, hey," like I was just fucking around. After that they left me alone but watched me. I wanted to cry, but I didn't. I just sat there doing my best to look catatonic until we docked and deboarded. I wanted to see a girl. A live one. Figured maybe I could get her to cry for both of us, and everybody else. Somebody ought to. Girls are better at it, since the guys' job is to join armies and frats and football teams and secret society death squad vigilante groups for the sole purpose of fucking with people. But I mean to put an end to that shit. I am the last asshole.

Rafe Vidrine

I went out to West Jeff to dig around for information about the Holt incident. I was mainly curious to see what cause of death was listed, if any.

The latest casualty of my failing eyesight was my driver's license—so I had Mattie drive me out. Which was fine, because Mattie behind the wheel insured that I would have a pleasant day no matter what, if anything, I turned up. Mattie's become my strongest tie to the living since Lauren passed. Problem is she's married, if not happily, at least comfortably (but probably happily, too).

We click, though. On the drive over to Petit Bois we got into a conversation about the weather. I remarked that much has been written about the effects on history of severe weather—the Russian Winter, the American Long Hot Summers—but almost nothing about the more temperate seasons. Today was a day you'd call balmy. Sixty-five degrees, breezy, golden slanting light with just the right degree of soft haze (Mattie filled in this last part). We called it a "lovely" day. But there is a sense on days such as this that something is hidden behind the breezes. Mattie agreed, adding that such days have a deceptive side, that while they encourage complacency, they also plant quiet seeds of fear that the day will be over, thus fostering a greater appreciation of mortal transience. The positive effect would be a heightened compassion for all living creatures, the downside a selfish and counter-productive hedonism. So I said, "Let's get a beer!" and we did.

After that, the bureaucratically vicious anonymity of the carpeted basement with its metal file cabinets seemed something like an abomination to me. I almost turned around and left without looking up anything. But Mattie had come down with me and she pressed me on.

We found Lucius Holt's death certificate and, as I suspected, the official cause of death was not entirely honest. It was listed as "exposure". The handwriting appeared so hurried that I pictured the coroner filling in a stack of them with his left hand while his right helped him to wolf down a hot sausage po-boy. I even looked for a mustard stain on the document. Couldn't find one. I was about to replace it in the drawer and get over to birth certificates when I noticed a different handwriting in the margins—a different language apparently, too. The ink as well as hand seemed contemporary, though. I handed it to Mattie, and she identified the language—Navajo!—but couldn't translate it (she's a Muskogean speaker, Chickasaw).

Muskogean would be more understandable. But Navajo? I suspected Loomis Mills, of course, but why would he commit such an incomprehensible act—and in such an indecipherable language? But my wonder was just proof of my recent synaptic incompetence. Absent-mindedness, a loathsome state. Mattie had to remind me that the girlfriend of Mills was in a summer program out on the Ship Rock Reservation (Navajo) when she was murdered.

That didn't explain too much, but the early data rarely does. I've sifted through piles and piles of documents on Alphonse Clouet, private and personal, yet he remains a massive question mark. Of course, he's dead and that gives me all the time in the world—not the case with Mills.

I'm tired. I want to sleep but I'm not sure what the effort will bring. I haven't told Mattie anything about my strange dream experiences yet. She asked me how the dreaming was going, but instead of lying outright, I spoke a subordinate truth: that my affections for Lauren wane in proportion to the days she stays dead, and that it makes a lot more sense to find living people to love. She said, "Thank you," then added, "for all of us."

Dearest Mills,

I hate it out here! It's not only boring, it's creepy.
Everybody looks at me weird. The Navajos are weird with
me because they can tell I'm not all white (I think)—and
they're **really** prejudiced against black people. Isn't that
funny? The other people around here are rednecks and
they hate me because they can tell I'm hip and they're
basically like the rednecks back home. Oh, there's stuck-
up artists, too. They're the ones that have all the fun but
they're rich snobs so you know what you'd say? "Fuck 'em,"
but when I say it you say "No, don't!" I miss those kinda
like just dumb conversations, though. I miss the intellectual conversations too, though. Remember we were going
to start that band and you came up with that name, the
U.R.T.I? Urban Radical Terrorist Intelligentsia? That was
fun. But it's not like that out here. Nobody's cool. The
family I'm living with is nice and all, but they're into God
big-time. They've got gospel music on the radio **all the
time**! They've got all these Navajo gospel bands, isn't that
funny?

Send me tapes! I know I don't have to tell you
about that special date coming up.

85

We're miles away from any real town out here. It's real **desert** for **miles**! I mean, it's beautiful, but it wears off. And sometimes it's creepy. I mean, I like woods better. We both do! But pretty soon I'm sure I'll get up into the mountains somehow and there's supposed to be nice trees and water up there. Speaking of water, there's **no** booze! Alcohol is illegal for anybody to have on the reservation! I know the Navajos are into pot, though (like everybody!), so I'm sure I'll hook up sooner or later. Of course I expect you to send me the **stuff** you **promised**! There's this one guy in our program who I think probably smokes up, but the rest of the Americans are all cubic zirconia.

I know there's Mexicans out here, too, but I haven't seen any. But I'd rather have to learn Spanish than Navajo! You have no idea. I can't imagine the first settler just sort of picking it up. Did you know that Navajo was the one code the Japanese could never break during World War II? It helped us win the war! I thought you'd like that tid-bit.

CRAZY! (that's my Mills expression for the day)

Hey, don't worry about me, really, it's just hard to get used to and changes are tough for me-you know that!-and I miss you!

Pleez pleez write me back?!?!

April XOXOX

Jessamine Marie DuClous Bascomb

An air of Mills Loomis Mills droops about me. I
suppose I have recently been or perhaps am even now in
his vicinity. Unfortunately, as I think you already know,
I have no means at my disposal accurately to verify matters of time, place, memory. As the currents of
brookwater through reeds and over stones are the fluc-
tuations of what we see and what we remember. Well do
I know this, yet, still, my shock at the memories Mills
Loomis Mills caused me to happen upon with his infer-
nal river ride was hurtsome indeed. Long unrecalled, this
place in myself should have been a flowery arbor in a
dessicated land, were it not for the cruel irony of their
association with such a brute as this Mills. But it was in
no degree a question of character that linked Mills with
visions of the first and only man to know me, it was
simply a matter of place and the elusive properties of the
air, whose moods are near infinite, and as unpredictable
as those of men, be they quick or dead.

It became salty somewhere, this bond tying me to
him, the redoubtable Captain Clouet, but then, on the
river, his muted emerald eyes, golden hand furled fingers
around the silver pheasant's head of his cane, soft lips

like a woman's, like his sister's, he had me in his thrall. What a silly girl I was. He spoke, "Jessamine, your hair the sable of a moonless night, your cheek the tender clouds of morning." Narcisse was a wooer.

I saw Loomis Mills, too, seating himself on the crude bench lining the starboard rail, he sat next to a boy who appeared lost and immediately set upon frightening the innocent child with his tales of an unhappy hereafter, "Can you smell the dead people—no, not their bodies, some of them give out a scent that you can track!" The boy tugged at his dungarees and looked up at the raving lunatic but once, then ran toward the comfort of his mother's skirts, causing her to spill some refreshment she had been drinking.

Of course Alphonse saw none of this. Yet, unlike Mills, he saw me. And unlike Mills, Alphonse saw no children, for it was an evening cruise with gambling and other mature entertainments. My mother had admonished me not to attend. Alas, however, my father trusted me then, and humored my peculiar curiosities. Ah, had I been born a boy-child, father and I might not have had to undertake our licentious wanderings so separately. Political men were always of special interest to me. My father recognized this and mistook it for love of him. So we each thoroughly enjoyed the political dinners we attended together, yet for different reasons. As for *ma mere*, as I was young and full of fire, I presumed to edify her as to the great world-shaking that was upon us—in our very city! I reminded her that we must all resolve to navigate the tides lest we be swept under by them. (This airing took place far from father's ears.) After the war such events became even more interesting to me, as we found ourselves at the tables of *gens de couleur*. Allowing Alphonse to take my hand thrilled me with a sense of myself as the most rakish Jacobin. But as he opened

my fingers and prepared his lips to press the warmth
of my open palm, my head lolled back upon my neck
and the sight of the black smoke gushing from the
twin chimneys of the boat caused me to cough and
shudder, to pull away from him.

The boat containing Mills became very small indeed, smaller than Alphonse's and my boat would ever
become, as it wended through the great ships which appeared like ominous sentries in the distant haze after one
of the bends of the river. The holds of these vessels might
contain whole forests of felled trees, enough brick and
iron to replace a city, and the weight to level it again.
The child whom Mills had previously tormented was
visibly afraid of them. Mills called them "tankers" and
told the child that these were not the boats to fear.

I recovered from the swoon caused by the sooty
coal smoke to discover Alphonse acting the part of the
rebuked suitor too easily. He threw his hand across his
temple and proclaimed, "I beg your pardon. I have been
too forward with a great lady who demands tact and patience. I beg you to understand that my political activities so often require swift and forceful action, in a world
where the timid are defeated. Ah, but now I bore you
with matters utterly trivial in the face of beauty, which
in this moment is the only matter of great consequence."

I hastened to inform him that I thought his political energies anything but trivial, that I rather admired
them, and then I saw the blush of his Gallic forebears
rise in his golden cheek.

"Mademoiselle, your flattery moves me. Have you
also an interest in affairs of state?"

I told him that my interest was great enough to
compel me daily to read Roudanez's *Tribune*. But at this
a cloud came over his face, and he replied with a low
grumble, "Ah, Roudanez!" I wondered why the name of
Louis Roudanez, one of his own class, after all, should

affect him so adversely, and so plainly; and my wonder only increased as he remained mute until we were called to supper in the stateroom. All my efforts at drawing a response from him proved fruitless, he would only shake his head and flourish his hand in an oratorical gesture whose meaning eluded me. At supper, as was to be expected, the *banal* tedium of table-talk ensued and subjects ranging in magnitude from the latest dresses to the latest hats were discussed without much animation from anyone—not from Alphonse, either, until his unexpected and unwelcome outburst. Taken in an objective light, it must be said, Clouet's temperament was fussy. He would sit sullen and refuse comment for, why, sometimes hours!

Loomis Mills passed the time, after seeming to reach some conclusion as to the unsatisfactoriness of the scenery outside, eating and conversing with the Negro manning the kiosk on the afterdeck. It did not surprise me in the least that Loomis Mills dined as one would expect a Mongol foot-soldier to. Like a dog bred for meanness on starvation rations, he grunted and allowed food to escape his mouth as he exhorted the vendor, "You oughta think about working on a dump like this. You think what you're doing here's helping the world? You oughta think again. You're part of the problem, man."

"What should I do to help the world, sir? Maybe there's some other job I ought to be doing?"

I see it clearly now: a waiter, in the narrow passage to the kitchen, tray in hand, of an exceedingly black hue, bald, Alphonse's hand upon his shoulder, engaged to all appearances in friendly conversation. It seemed from the floridness of their faces they must be speaking French. One's face opens to the world when one speaks French— so unlike the tight-lipped English. What are they discussing? This preoccupied me throughout dinner. I was unable to give an opinion on whether feathers, and what shade, belonged in ladies' hats. The men stood and spoke, in the stiffest formality, of more pressing matters, with raised glasses. Alphonse's comments were not pleasing to my father.

"Among the white men of this country," he declaimed, "there are great differences in intelligence, character, no?" He was careful not to allow time for reflection, hastening to add, "So it is, too, among the Negro race. In fact, it would appear that culture and education are far clearer determinants of refinement than shades of flesh. Why the preoccupation with the accidents of skin color? It demeans the noble ancestries of all. I, myself," he raised his voice and held captive with his eyes the entire assembly, "I, myself, contain the heated passions of the untamed African in my blood." At this he paused and seemed to measure off in his head a proper interval, then he added what was clearly intended to soften his previous suggestion, which all present had seemed to find threatening. "Yet the uncivilized African is also impressionable, and possesses a love of life and of God which is unrivaled by any nation of the wide world. I thank God for the African in me—however limited the strain—because it enables me better to understand and direct those untrammeled African children so now in need of guidance." He raised his glass, but only the priest drank with him. The others wore that subtle set of mouth in an attitude so familiar to me, but which seemed foreign or yet invisible to Narcisse. So he continued, "Yet I thank God also for the Frenchman in me, who taught me love of art and beauty." At this he bowed his head at me, and indicated the canvases adorning the room with a sweeping gesture of his hand. The qualified amusement of the other guests departed as subtly as it had begun. Their stiffening could be felt if not observed with the eye. I was most careful to steer my gaze far from Bascomb, my father. "And," Clouet amended, "for the Anglo-Saxon, to whose thrift and industry it is due that I find myself seated here among the truly great men of our city." I had not been aware of any Anglo-Saxon lineage. It was no doubt fabricated for the occasion. He allowed a moment for his awkward flattery to make everyone feel ill at ease, and then stood and lifted his glass higher and more demonstrably than previously, "In the coming generations we must insure that the freedmen learn the ways of our democracy under orderly and compassionate guidance! I praise the men seated here, who have pledged their assistance to those of us whom God saw fit generations ago to prepare for the momentous undertaking of representing the newest citizens of Louisiana and of the United States of America!"

Mills stop you're so funny I hate you all of you if there's a hell.

The new girl bleeds again. If I could but hold her to my breast.

Father Miguel De Rozas was the most enthusiastic respondent. He upset his wineglass in his haste to rise and applaud. Others followed suit, but not all. The most conspicuous skeptics were the yankee sent to represent General Banks, and Pinchback. His words, spoken *sotto voce* to me, seated nearest him, were succinct: "We shall see." Cigars were drawn, but Alphonse's longed-for approbation was prevented by an announcement that the Tchefuncte River approached, and that the alligators were plentiful. The men readied their firearms and all proceeded to the starboard rail.

Mills Loomis Mills balanced himself most awkwardly upon it, his torso angling forward, then back, as startled passengers stood aghast, paralyzed at the sight of his wild-eyed enthusiasm for death. Would he had plunged into the swirling eddies below.

With the aid of directed lanterns, the eyes of the alligators were made to reflect back what resembled evenly set pairs of red embers, moving slowly to and fro as they swam. This rendered the creatures easy targets, and the firing commenced. The smoke from the Winchesters, in collusion with the stillwater's reflection of a dark sky, shining like black glass, caused me to swoon. Sight and memory both began a rapid disintegration into a black thickness—accompanied by a drone as of bagpipes—and my fears about the purpose of Mills' river excursion were confirmed, for it was soul resin that upset me so. It threatened to banish me to my most deleterious moments, where exist no sometime lovers, no Aphonse Clouet, no Reina Clouet, no scenery, no sylphs, no memory of balmy breeze. Just me, just awful me.

Mills Loomis Mills

When they docked a couple of overgrown Boy Scouts accosted me walking down the plank. They'd been watching me ever since I danced on the rail. They asked did I have a place to go, which was hilarious because it was obvious what they really wanted to do was beat the shit out of me for being a freak (or lock me up). I laughed at them and told them to relax and convinced them I was a happy normal guy. I told them I had one too many reefers before I got on the boat and that seemed to set them at ease.

I walked through and past the Quarter, Canal Street, kept going till the last tourist receded and it was obviously slum. A huge barn of a church rose up out of a sea of beat-up leaning shotgun shacks either shut up tight or with the doors hanging open pushing darkness, coolness, and TV out onto the glaring sidewalk. I knew there had to be payphones in a neighborhood like this. I wound around until I reached the giant church, and sure enough, there was a payphone growing out of a shaded, littered patch of dirt right next to it. The door to the sanctuary was open and I snuck a peek and there he was, nailed up with gory blood streaming off of him. Catholics. Instead of drinking His blood they should offer some of their own once a week. I bet that's how they started out though. The ancient people knew about stuff like that. Knew about blood. Knew about soul resin.

I used my last fifty cents to call an old friend, somebody who I knew would appreciate my accomplishments. He answered the phone the way I knew he would: "Rafe Vidrine."

I snickered and said, "Rafe Vidrine, huh? Guess I got the right place."

"Loomis Mills?"

"What, are you clairvoyant now?"

"Actually, I think I may be."

"Doesn't sound like a very scientific opinion."

"What science have you been up to lately?"

He seemed to know too much. Not from what he said, but his tone, sounded urgent or something. But there's no way. All he knew was that I freaked out a little at school and dropped out.

I said normal stuff like, "Well, it's taken me awhile to grieve—I know you know why I had to take a break from college. I'm pretty much all together now though. Thinking about coming back maybe next semester. Teaching anything good?"

"My Reconstruction seminar. But I—"

"Yeah? Write any good books about it lately?"

"No books. I had been working on an article, but I've been distracted lately…"

He just kind of trailed off. Like he was thinking how to trap me with some statement. But I wanted to get him. I said, "What's the article about?"

"Oh, a biographical piece about one of the players—"

"Who? Which one?"

"I'm not sure you would have—"

"Alphonse Clouet?"

Then he really stopped talking. I sat there listening to him not breathing for musta been a whole minute. Then he said, "A pretty incredible guess, you know about him, I suppose?"

"Not really. I don't know, the name just came to me. He must be in the Foner book, or the Blassingame—"

"He's not in either."

How did *he* end up snagging *me?* I really didn't know where I pulled that name from. But obviously I must've read it somewhere. He was lying about the books—or getting too old to remember. Or lying about that being somebody's real name in the first place. I said, "But really, that's a real guy?"

"Was." Silence. The "rhetorical" kind.

So I said, "I'm leaving town soon, getting out to New Mexico to do some archaeology."

"In Navajo country?"

He was trying to toy with me some more. No dice. "No. Apache."

"But you speak Navajo?"

"Who does really? You been out to Petit Bois lately?"

"Yes. You, too."

"Yeah. So you know I've been doing my research. That's what I called you about. Before I head out west I wanna hand in that paper and clean up that incomplete."

"You find Lucius Holt?"

"Yeah."

Jessamine Marie DuClous Bascomb

Dine bizaad bohoosh'aah. Haash yinilye.

I confess I have no hope for the Indian girl my *sylphide* has brought along with her. I know she is Indian from her dress only, and from her manner of speaking, with the aid of grunts and lip-smacking. But her shade is exceedingly faint—as if she doesn't belong here at all, as if she is not one of us, but rather simply an apparition.

Haash yinilye? April yinishye. April yinishye.

I fancy she speaks of April. Who would not like to? It puts me in mind of a soiree at the Clouet residence, a place marked by an ostentation which would feign rival the Palazzo of the Doges. Well, in the interior only, with its marble mantels, brass andirons, plenitude of silver, damask, and painted canvasses in heavy gilt frames. The exterior was a trifle forlorn, even if grand in its proportions. The house sat high off the ground, on fifteen-foot pillars. A broad stair, replete with gracefully curving balustrades, led up to the wide gallery, which circled the entire structure. Out of the slate roof rose a white-fenced belvedere, commanding vistas of cathedral and river.

April is a flowery month, then as now, and all the leading lights of the flowery kingdom were in attendance on that April evening on the Elysian Fields. Much time must have elapsed since the Captain first emboldened himself to grasp my hand. Perhaps in that time political influence—probably among the Negro element of the new *gendarmes*—had made Clouet yet bolder. But, on this night at least, his worldly victories moved me but little to give myself up to him. In fact, though he undoubtedly derived his own pleasure from the incident, it mattered little to me that the man was he. On a starlit April veranda, after the *Nocturnes* of Chopin, after fine red *Bordeaux*, French society, Swiss chocolate? Who could do otherwise? Whether he was affectionate and tender, I do not recall. The breezes were, and that was my principal delight. Given the opium in the air of the azaleas, verbena, wisteria, sweet olive, and, of course, cape jessamine? It had perhaps been wiser for me to taste the oleander blossom rather than Clouet's silken flesh, so like woman's. Clouet departed, however, and, as clearly as I remember, I see the April bouquet still blooms—though the stars have long since fled the city. Consider then, before you cast stones, who it was who truly took and embraced me that night, Clouet or the perfumed air? I say it was the worthier. And the turbulent portion of my life which must surely have followed on the heels of that fateful night, I dedicate it, too, to the unassuming grace of vines and cultured bushes, but especially to the sweetest *fleur* of all, Reina, whom I never would have known did I not permit myself license regarding her brother.

However, it is not for any romantic impropriety that I am forced to do penance here.

Then, of course, none of us really knows.

Rafe Vidrine

Mills' phone-call righted the fabrication I'd produced for the police, but I couldn't say I found what he
said threatening to my person. How'd he know about
Clouet? He'd probably gotten a hold of one of my books.
There were any number of places where he could have
seen Clouet's name, really. It came up frequently, if not
favorably. I might wonder why he seemed to assume that
I would give a damn enough to follow his movements,
but I know he suffers from megalomaniac delusions,
which explains it.

No, what got to me more was an anonymous
typed postcard I'd gotten the day before which I now
knew to connect to Mills. It was one of those picturing an alligator opening its mouth behind a kneeling
bikini-clad unsuspecting woman. On the back was this:

*"I know I'm supposed to say, 'I'm OK, you're
OK,' but I can't. I'm not. We're not. We're not OK.
'Watchman, what of the night? Watchman, what of the
night?'"*

— Jimmy Swaggart, Sermon of 6/23/96

Mills Loomis Mills

Sometimes I remember talking to him, remember phrases, his tone of voice like yuppie salad dressing with tarragon floating in it in a slim corked bottle. He had a smell, too, a mix of girl's perfume that I'm sure he wore himself. That would have been fine, but on top of that was dirty body, and bad fart, or even shit, the sick acrid drunk or too much coffee kind. But other times I don't remember anything, I just know that I know more than I did when I went to sleep. It's like a beeping light on an answering machine in my brain. So I wait for the message to brew itself up. That's another thing the Buddha knew about: you don't find something by going out and looking for it, you wait for it to come to you. Like on the Mississippi Belle, I wasn't directly looking for something, I was putting myself in the general area of something (a big thing) and letting it put itself around me.

But also, after I came down a little bit from the high I'd been riding from being on the river and the resin and Holt and the whole…just all of it, I got a little creeped out. I started to wonder why there are people at all, and I hate wondering that. It makes me feel like I'm some kind of a traitor.

So I wandered the streets for a while coming across blood sounds here and there but letting them lie. I tried to horn in on a couple of parties, but I didn't get very far. I came across a clump of black folks on the corner by a grocery store, but they ignored me after a couple polite nods and amused stares. Then I ran into a mixed-race set of bums sitting on and leaning against a low stone wall by the statue of a WWI guy lobbing a grenade. They were fine on me hanging with them at first. I got a gulp of Katz and Bestoff vodka out of it, but that's where the generosity ended. They let me stand there next to them, but the bottle never went my way again. They were older than me, so they didn't trust me. Then I remembered something Vidrine said back in college. He said America was a clique society. Depending on class and culture, the American guy had a small range of freedom in choosing his own scene, defined by fashion, art and music taste, etc., but more and more by generation. See, I learned lots of useful stuff in college. I applied the principle by walking in the direction where I knew there were lots of young college dropout burnouts that I knew would tolerate me if I played it right. I knew there was no way to continue fighting the good fight without a couple of good beers and a couple of pieces of pizza or burger or fried chicken. Sure enough, after the post-industrial bum, druggie 'n ho strip came a thin belt of black old-people shotgun housing followed by the run-down but pretty abodes of the white stoners. Sagging porches with hammocks, lots of plants, bright cloths (not curtains) blowing out of open windows, bamboo windchimes. I knew I was set when I saw it up on the grass by a peeling pink camelback: a ten year-old Volvo station wagon with decals on the rear window of dancing multi-colored bears and the bloated skull with the lightning bolt. Deadheads. Bingo.

Deadheads are good people, maybe the best people. They're open and they're ready to hear just about any-thing. And that's great because while I was kicking back I could also throw stuff at them gradually, about my plan. I mean 'cause I'm gonna need at least one of them eventually. I said "hey man" to a hairy guy grabbing an excellent-looking wet green bottle out of a cooler on the porch. I said, "Damn, that looks good." He just said yep and settled back on a chewed-up easy chair. I told him I lived down the street and didn't they just move in and how did they like the neighborhood. Smart bet. I got invited to sit around and drink a few cold ones. The commercial's right: it doesn't get any better than that.

A pretty girl came around, too. She caused me to doubt. We all went inside and watched TV, and I real-ized that even though it might be bad that beer and TV are about the most sublime thing most people ever experience, it ain't that bad, either. We were chilling out on the old comfy alley furniture, and they had all the doors and windows open, and it rained and that was nice. All they had in the living room was a couple of old alley couches and a stopsign on milk crates for a bong-table. And posters and some sleeping bags and pillows on the floor for dogs or people to lie on. Nice state-of-the-art TV, too, of course, with cable. Everything else was just beer bottles (good beer) and drug stuff. We were watching *Kung Fu* and a com-mercial came around (which they were always smart enough to mute), and I said, "You don't find some-thing by going out and looking for it, you find it by just waiting for it to find you."

They all said, "Whoa!" and "Straight, man" and the girl said "Wow!"

One of 'em, though, didn't like me, and I was just waiting for him to get smart. He wasn't planning on it right then, though, 'cause he was too busy salivating over the sheet of blotter I was laying on them all. All he had to say was, "Let's dose, man." The acid was at least three years old and had gotten wet whenever my pack got soaked in the rain, but hey, they didn't know all that history.

I guess I should have known that I might end up losing it—my composure—before the night was over. Camaraderie can do it to you, but what's a man supposed to do? Steer clear of people forever? Impossible. Like the girl, Maya, she was cute and nice and smiled plenty and laughed a lot. I liked her and I wanted to skip off, holding hands with her. But I never planned to hit on her or anything because she was supposed to be the girlfriend of this other guy, Limerick (yeah, he's a joke, all right), and it's not like I liked him or anything, but he was being a friend, I guess, inviting me into his home like Christians claim they used to do. The stuck-up guy's name was Charles—even his name was stuck-up—and he was sitting there on a sleeping bag being all nice with everybody, but whenever I said something was the *only* time he didn't have something to say. He'd just nod, and maybe do a "mmmm." Like he thought he was some professor.

I guess that's all who was there—Limerick, Charles and Maya. I thought there was more, but I guess not. Oh yeah, that old me who showed up and embarrassed contemporary me (funny how that happens to people and countries). But old embarrassing sentimental me didn't show up 'til later so I was OK for most of the night. It wasn't only the nice pretty girl that brought me down, or the extended period spent hanging with normal people who are friendly and have no clue about the screaming blood saturating the air they breathe every second. It was also because of the acid. I didn't do any—I'm way past that—but them being on it was enough.

The TV should've helped but it didn't. Another commercial came around, and I said, "Kung Fu there, he's got a lot of wisdom because why? Well, he knows that the place he keeps roaming around in isn't something simple like a geographical region, like the Old West between 1865 and 1890—he knows that what it is is what they call a *trans-historical constant.* It's like a mental space, but one that gets shared by lots of people because check it out: aren't they all already ghosts by the time we're watching this now?"

Limerick just went, "Whoa," but Maya said, "You say the strangest things. That's cool."

Mmm. She was tugging at my heartstrings, those old frayed anchor-wielding deadbeats.

Charles: nothing. But when Maya pointed at the TV and said, "Isn't that those new fruity cocktails in the painted bottles?" Charles piped up—"Yeah, *Beach Breezes.* They're taking a big gamble. Remember *Zima?* That didn't pan out. Of course lots of beer alternatives have been pretty successful, like the wine coolers—but of course that was temporary, too. The Jack Daniels Country Cocktails, though, and the Jim Beam and cokes in the can have been doing pretty well."

I couldn't take it, I said, "Total pesky miniscule meaninglessness. The point in this case is the alcohol, right? Who the hell cares what form it comes in, what the fucking package looks like?"

Charles ignored me. Got up to get a beer, of all things. And Limerick followed him. Their plan was to talk about me and sure enough, I heard them laughing. Yeah, the freak is so funny, can't understand the profundity of a Jack Daniels label. But that left me and Maya sitting there (which I later figured out had to happen, like the invention of the lightbulb or the discovery of America). She was a pale short wispy blackhaired mouse with a hard loud voice. She said, "Y'know I agree with you. I've thought about that before, too, but nobody else ever said anything. You're right, it doesn't matter. I mean the package doesn't, but what about the taste, does the taste matter?"

I had to think about that one. And when I thought about it I saw that it was a really good question. I knew it was good because I couldn't answer it. So I was honest. I said, "Maybe. Maybe it does, maybe it doesn't."

That's when she blew me away and threw the monkey wrench into everything I'd been putting together— my theories. She said, "I guess it depends on whether you're thinking about the future or about the present."

It hurt me, but I guess in a good way, because it made me realize that I should take the present more seriously, like, because the present is real, too. But I came up with a reply for her, and I could tell it reached her: "But is there any present at all? Isn't it all maybe just past and future?"

Then Limerick and Charles came back and Charles started talking about some TV show he didn't think deserved to be on TV. He said it was "derivative." Charles is not a true Deadhead. Too many ideas. The wrong ones, though. TV? C'mon, who the hell cares? I said that. I said it would be more productive to talk about Matchbox racing cars.

Around about then they started to trip and got quiet—I knew they were on the upswing. Maya was the first one to get out of herself. She started talking: "Like so Kung Fu is in this space that's a real historical space but also a space that's left there, that's gone out on its own and made its own life but wasn't he drinking a Jack and Coke in that episode? Doesn't that make it like not that space away from everything and more like it's like part of this same layer that we're in? But the coke isn't really part of our layer, either, we're just supposed to think it is 'cause…"

"'Cause they want us to," I said.

Limerick said, "Yeah, man. They do. And they do this other thing, too, this..." but he lost the flow and stopped. Probably a few sentences ahead.

Maya didn't really ever stop, she kept going in her circle, she was walking in a circle, too, "A coke'd be good right now, though. But it's got caffeine and that's not cool. A beer's the thing to have, right. I'm gonna go get one. Yeah, that'll be cool! So if Kung Fu can have a coke— like he did, right?—but it's more likely they'd have beer back then. So would he have a Jack and coke? He couldn't have it in those cans 'cause they didn't do it that way, then. But he wasn't really *then*. But not now, either, 'cause they're re-runs. So they were actually done in the past and David Carradine is an older guy now, but for him, he doesn't remember the episodes, he just remembers doing stuff around them, but all Kung Fu remembers is the episodes 'cause those are the only times he ever existed. And he's a ghost now—but he was always a ghost because that place he lived in wasn't really the Wild West, it was just one that was in the imagination. But his or ours or somebody else's? Is that all a ghost is, just something in the imagination?"

I said, "Yes and no," and she got up to get a coke, then sat down and changed her mind—decided to go with beer instead—and got up again and started walking, then turned back and said to me, "What did you say?"

"I said, 'yes and no,' about ghosts being in the imagination. Think about it: how else could a ghost reach you except through your imagination? But that doesn't mean they don't exist, it just means that the Old Science has taught us to call lots of stuff 'imagination' that never used to be—anything you can't pick up in your hand or get something material out of, anything you can't buy—like a coke."

"Coke is definitely not a ghost thing."
"Well, they can't drink it, but they might want one."
"She says she doesn't."
"What?"
"She doesn't want one."
"What does she want?"
"A beer."
"A beer? I'll get you one. I'll actually make it to the kitchen and back."

I went to get the beer and Charles was back there with his palms flat on the countertop like he was lifting himself up in some exercise. He was totally checking out the pattern in the formica. I said, "Jack Daniel's Country Cocktail don't seem too relevant, now, huh?"

He didn't say anything, but he did look at me. He was scared. And that made me scared because I knew my trip wasn't just going to be "a passage of time," like trippers say. I told him about his, though, said, "It's a passage of time," handed him a cold beer, then took it back and opened it for him (I saw his eyes start the trip back already right then). I said, "Open up, man, start talking, it'll bring you out."

And I knew talking would never bring me out. And I started to slack on my resolve. Started to think my own present was more important than everybody's future. Then the worst: that maybe I was wrong about the whole plan. But hey, remember Jesus himself wanted to back down at the last minute, too. I'm not comparing myself or anything, I'm just saying, we should all strive to be like Him, right? So, come jitters or whatever, I'll drink my cup when the time comes.

But why I want to procrastinate should be clear. The problem I have at this stage is this: the old blood which is the soul resin needs to be activated. With what? Not some mumbo-jumbo voodoo hocus pocus abracadabra. What do you think? With blood, Sherlock. Fresh,

warm, living, heart-pumped human blood. On site.
That's my problem.

I went back up front and Maya was still talking—to
nobody, Limerick was out on the front porch lying on
his back looking at roaches or whatever on the bottom
side of the awning. I thought about dragging him over a
foot or so, so he could at least see the sky, but Limerick
is an old hand and knows what he wants. I handed the
open beer to Maya, but she didn't seem to recognize it as
something she wanted. I said, "Didn't she want a beer?"

"No, she wants coffee and eggs with anchovies
in it."

A tripper would never ask for something like that.
It was somebody from over there. They had her. Not
Maya.

One time when me and April were living together
we were out of almost everything to eat, and we were
sick of just eating plain eggs over and over again, so
we made scrambled eggs with anchovies. Even though
I know a scientist is supposed to be distant and pro-
fessional, I was truly freaked out. I said to Maya, "What?
Eggs and what?"

But she was further down the cycle—talking about
David Carradine again—and I had to get alone fast so
I wouldn't lose control in front of the trippers and
bum them out. I went out back and sat on a cooler
and turned the porchlight out. I found that place, went
right to it, to get it over with. Put me in the kitchen
with April and her doing her humming routine she
always did when she watered the plants, saw her wres-
tling on the floor with 'Shoba, saw her touching my
face saying, "Are you OK?" and eyebrows up and down
with smirk undoing her blouse. And it came, what I
was looking for, pathetic curled-up animal-groaning
sob session. People have to do it, cry, and when they
don't they're sorry they didn't (Jesus did, he "wept").

So the best thing is to get it out discreetly in one big pour.

But Maya fucked up my plan again, she tracked me down and put her hand on me, and said it just like *she* used to, "Are you OK?" And I wondered where the present was and who the hell was talking to me.

Rafe Vidrine, from Discriminate Mob: The American Race Riot, 1863-1992

By the summer of 1866 the tension in New Orleans was thick enough to be palpable to visitors. A *New York Times* reporter dispatched his take on the mood of the city on July 4: "The people here are more bitter than in any place I have yet found." The *Chicago Tribune* reported on the state of affairs leading up to July 30: "Pistols were purchased in large numbers, and everybody seemed preparing." The radical move to reconvoke the state constitutional convention had the support of a frustrated and isolated governor Wells, but not of the men who had elected and grown fed up with him. The idea may have had the tacit support of the radical Republican coalition in the U.S. Congress, but not of the President, Andrew Johnson, who had proven much more conciliatory to the "rebel" element than the radicals imagined Lincoln would have been.

Legitimate questions about the legality of a new convention added the fuel of righteousness to many ex-Confederates who truly saw the push for black enfranchisement as a draconian revenge measure rather than as a necessary move toward building a new, more democratic South. It may well have seemed so to them since only five northern states, all in New England, allowed blacks to vote on equal terms with whites. The opportunistic alliance between the conservative Governor Wells and the radicals he had, until recently, vehemently opposed, would fit nicely into later Redeemer myths of Reconstruction. To the "rebel gentlemen" it seemed an unholy marriage between fanatical ideologues and a self-serving politico hungry for power. Indeed, it may have been true that the promise of black suffrage was incidental to Wells' personal aims.

Yet, incidental or not, the dream of political equality stirred the emotions and ambitions of New Orleans' continuously swelling black population. They would be outside the convention hall in force and armed, to face the police force of Governor Wells' political enemy, New Orleans Mayor Hugh Kennedy. On Friday July 27, three days before the contested convention was to sit, meetings and a public rally were held at the convention site, the Mechanic's Institute, which stood in the block bounded by Common, Baronne, Dryades, and Canal. The primary aim of the many speeches delivered seems to have been to impress upon the freedmen the importance of the new convention for their interests. They were exhorted in general to make their support of a new constitution known, though the speakers differed in how this support should best be demonstrated. The speaker who made the biggest impression, according to military and congressional reports inquiring into causes of the July 30 riot, was Alphonse Clouet, who was broadly accused of having resorted to incendiary rhetoric. An enemy of the convention paraphrased Clouet's words thus:

> The very stones of the streets of New Orleans
> cry for the blood of these traitors, these rebels.
> We shall have a meeting here on Monday, in this

hall in the second story, come armed; we want no cowards, come armed; if any white man molest you knock him down.

A more neutral source was a reporter for the *New York Weekly Tribune*, who testified that Clouet

> congratulated the Negroes on having conducted
> themselves so very quietly and orderly during
> the evening. He recommended them to go quietly
> to their homes. If they were assaulted and
> knocked down by anyone he would advise them to
> defend themselves, and if necessary to save
> their own lives to kill the party who assaulted
> them.

The Saturday morning after the rally, the arch-conservative French-language New Orleans *Bee* and its anglophone counterpart, *New Orleans Times*, both said only of Clouet's speech that he had advised the freedmen to kill any white men who "molested" them.

Yet however inflammatory Clouet's words may have been, they did not result in violence the night they were spoken. The only incident on Friday was a brief melee between a handful of blacks and white onlookers, sparked when a little white girl said, too audibly, "Look, mommy, there goes a nigger with a flag!"

Jessamine Marie DuClous Bascomb

My father would have had my head, of course, had
he ever known of the extent of my association with
Narcisse. As it was, I am more than certain that father
was among the men who attempted to extinguish Clouet's
rising star before the Mechanic's Institute during that
dreadful summer, and I know equally well that he led
the brigands who fired on Clouet's militia at Liberty Place
many summers later. They were all Pickwick Club men.
I knew of their intrigues, indeed, I do not doubt that
everyone knew. But now I count it among my regrets
that I never disclosed to father real details of my own
nocturnal outings. For himself, he never forcefully inquired after them, either. I suspect this is because his dal-
liances may have been more potentially upsetting to the
laws of man and God, and to my mother, than were mine.
Our coaches no doubt crossed paths on many a moonless night. Certainly many a wink and nod were passed
between us in the corridors of our...that is to say my
father's home. It was in Harmony Street. So my father
called it "Harmony Home," though it would know no
harmony, it would learn only plainchant, when the one
voice alone was left—his.

I remember one morning, perhaps the last of its kind, the sun had already climbed a few cloudy stairs. General Bascomb, my father, reclined indolently on the hewn-log bench—some relic of the Bascombs' former humility—on our front porch. He had removed his left leg—also hewn out of wood—and it was the first time I had seen it independently of him since his return from Vicksburg, where he had acquired this piece of practical craftsmanship. I discerned well before our obligatory filial embrace that he had whiled away the night hours over at Pope's drugstore, quaffing liberally from the jug and plotting against the legal regime of our State. Hence I knew more of his nocturnal wanderings than he did of mine, as I straightaway learned. For clutching his false leg and starting up suddenly upon the flesh one, he railed, "Would that the Frenchman had not been conceived by Him above, and that the French woman not been sheltered by me here below! Still, there are things in our less glorious world which even God Almighty can't help a lick."

I strove to bypass him with a tact not warranted by his own impertinence—for although I always did and will ever love my mother, I never held like sentiments for my father, respect him as I must. I excused myself and stooped to retrieve my strategically loosed vinaigrette, thus contriving to step up again behind him. But he had not imbibed quite as much as I had imagined or hoped. On single foot and cane he spun around to face me once more. His prosthesis he disdainfully flung at my feet. He let his cane fall then, too, gripping my shoulders as his only means of balance. I do remember my great hope that it might be my last look into that face, with its porcine pink devoid of lips, eyelashes, or any other feature of beauty. Struggling to hold himself erect, he sputtered into my hair, for my face was turned in revulsion, "That miserable stump of a tree which I adorn the stump of my body with, 'twas for you I thought I earned it! You and your ill-made mother, whose eyes—for her tongue has long since expired—have only contempt for my sacrifices!" He spat and winced. "Nothing ever but we'll get them yet." Ah, my American father, eloquence never attended you.

I fancy he weeps, but I will never weep for him, rather would I pay the eternal price for father-hatred.

"You, a Frenchwoman like your dam—madame, I should say?—well enough you seem to know the fire of youth as only a black-haired DuClous can learn it." He grins now as would a cardsharp with a cuffed ace. "But you will see, the same inner extinguishment which afflicts your mother will strike you; it may well be a scientific inevitablity. For you love the night too much, and the elixirs of the night that I pray to God are served only in fluted glasses, not silk pillows…in that respect at least you may be an improvement on the other female who shares my roof."

and 'Shoba came running up the mesa and he barked like Lassie and it was all over but it wasn't all over and 'Shoba wasn't there Mills doing his funny walk like the Dr. Mario germs and doing the music and coming after me in the kitchen but it wasn't Mills and it wasn't funny

He bowed his head as before the funeral train of Madame Beauregard. I sought to speak in the opportune interval. However, hardly had I expressed my great fatigue when he callously shushed me and continued. "As you clearly prefer the Latin Districts to our neighborhood, please go reside there. I have room here for but one who cares not for the name Bascomb."

"Father?"

Yes, perhaps this was the first day of my second, dearest and most hurried life. Yet I still cannot say whether that—final?—chapter would best be likened to unfurling morning-glory or uncoiling adder.

"It is fortuitous that you have extended your Bacchanale to such a late, that is, early hour. I am sure Mr. Peters will be available if you call at Whitney's Bank— I have no doubt that you would prefer a moneyhouse with a Gallic name, but unfortunately your people have not excelled in the matter of solvent industry." He fell back onto the log in order to use his own hand to take from his pocket a sealed letter, which he instructed me to deliver to Mr. Peters. All that was left to the business was his suggestion that I take the trolley, and an intimation that I should feel myself most at home there.

Mom quit partying and then she got meaner than she ever used to be. She said how doing illegal stuff means you meet illegal people and you could get hurt and if what you're doing's against God the hurt will never heal

My dear sylph, I must honestly counsel you that the admonition to love one's father and mother without demand of reciprocity is a baseless vanity of the fathers and mothers themselves. Yes, the mother must suffer to bring forth the child, but this suffering was not ordained by her offspring. And as for the father, he has no role in the matter save the satisfaction of his own brute lusts. As for me, I was happy to have an end to the stinging discomfiture of Bascomb's "fatherly attentions".

Reverend Vidrine?

"Yes?"

You are a man of God, sir?

"No. Men. History. I teach, write."

How well suited you are, then. The child's name is April, and she knew Mills Loomis Mills.

"And you?"

Do you not remember our other conversations?

"No. Just seeing you."

Rafe Vidrine

When Mattie LaVonne and I met for lunch on the 12th, I had already decided to come clean with her about the turn my dreams had taken. The disconcerting satin-clad woman stalked around in them all the time now. Mattie and I met at a new restaurant on Elysian Fields. The place had gotten some good reviews, but I was more interested in its location—on or near the site where the Clouet mansion had once stood. Mattie seemed younger, bouncier, than she'd been, I thought, in a long time. Her silver-streaked black hair wasn't in its usual practical ponytail or bun, but up, with class and grace and a silver comb. Her workday rimless glasses were gone. I saw there were contacts on her clear light brown eyes. Why? For me?

We were situated nicely on the patio, waiting for drinks. I was opening my mouth to confess that my dreams had gotten out of my control, but she got there first: "You've encountered something in your dreaming, haven't you?"

I said yes and asked how she had guessed it.

"It can happen that a particularly perceptive, intuitive person can have so much success in dreaming that…well, that they make space for it—for dreaming—during waking."

"Daydreaming?"

"That's different. You can call it dreaming during the day, though."

"Maybe as an effect of old age, maybe…senility?" I hoped I made the sarcasm clear enough. I felt a rush of embarrassment, though, because my voice had been raised in mock surprise and there the waiter suddenly stood. I waited for him to give us our drinks and move on, or ask us to order, or anything at all. But he just stood there, mute. He scratched his head aimlessly and then yanked at his hair, grimacing as if it hurt. I made eye contact, "Yes?"

And Mattie said, "Who are you talking to now, for example?"

I turned to Mattie and when I looked back, the waiter had vanished—or faded or walked off or something. Maybe vanished: Mattie hadn't seen him at all.

"I'm not calling you senile. It's quite the opposite, I think. Senile means a dulling of the mind, forgetting things."

"I am doing that."

"Not enough. You're an absent-minded professor, and so, like a cliché, have become a parody of the normal."

I was feeling more confident than I had in months, but I wanted to play hurt to see how Mattie would react. So I said, "Are you calling me a cliché or a parody—I don't think the terms are the same, but I don't care to rank them." I looked away from her and sipped beer. It was wonderful, a rich dark porter. But I hadn't noticed anybody putting it there.

"Don't play hurt with me, Rafe." Her smile was broad and a flash was in her eyes again.

I said, "Baton twirler," and thought, giddy, "on a merry-go-round with me." I then wondered what I was saying and why.

She laughed, I don't think uncomfortably, but she did seem startled.

I said, "Where were we—my dreams, right?"

"Yes," still smiling, "the ones you have while you're sleeping."

"But you said it's the same during the day."

"No. I asked. You never answered."

I nodded and we both seemed to realize how serious things might be, how cautiously our words should be chosen, given their likely consequences. Mattie's face suddenly sagged into creases, and I saw that she worried for me: the end? A last irrational flourish before death? Was this the cause of her new, more flirtatious way with me? I'm not sure I cared about the why, though. It's supreme to feel desired when you assumed the last dance had been over a long time ago.

"It's not about Lauren anymore, is it?"

I wondered how she meant the question. But my flash of sobriety told me it was about the dreaming. I said, "Jessamine."

"What?"

I felt a distinct physical sensation, like a thing brushing past some organ inside me. Like a heart flutter, but an invigorating one. Like a shot of coffee after a long sleep. A face came to mind, remembered from a recent passing glance or from a deep relationship ages ago. I thought back to college, grad school.

I said, "That's who I dream about," and realized it was true, that I dreamed about her. Then I realized I had just uttered her name. Again: "Jessamine."

"Is that a woman?"

I could barely even see Mattie anymore. Again, the puke smell, but I'd gotten used to it.

"Who is she?"

"Well, she used to spend some time right around here." I waved my hand up and down at the street through the grating in the brick wall of the patio—the corner of Elysian Fields and Clouet. I heard the fountain behind me and wondered whether it had been there when we came in. I was beginning to understand. Why had I really wanted to eat at a place near the site of Alphonse Clouet's former residence? Not for any conventional research purposes. How do I know what he looked like. *How do I know what he looked like?* No authenticated portraits exist. He had a pheasant's head on his favorite cane, because pheasant was his favorite fowl. For hunting and eating. Where had I read that?

I said, "Jessamine Marie DuClous Bascomb."

"Cryptic Rafe Vidrine Obscurant."

"She's...she's, I think she's dead."

"Rafe..."

I was committed to explaining everything in detail to Mattie, but things were rushing past me too quickly to speak—names...*people.* My mind and body felt like a computer booting up. I heard little buzzes and clicks inside myself, lights coming on. I said, "Lord in Heaven...Nash Newton Bascomb."

"Rafe?"

"The daughter, Jessamine Marie..."

And there she was, rippling into view. Standing. Dark, draping, crinkling dress, shawl trailing off of her shoulders, not budging in the strong breeze that blew my napkin off the table. Buskin boots. Black wisps of hair cloying to her antiqued ivory skin, pearls, wrists, cameo choker, jet hair, white, veined marble cheeks and temples. Her arms were extended, like an invitation, a friendly one, as if waving me out to the porch for ice-coffee. I saw all this, but her image came through like a wavy silt formation under several feet of clear but swift water. I felt an urge to dive and touch my face to hers. But I just as quickly recoiled. She had vomit, bloody vomit, down her chin and neck, and the glassy gray of her eyes unsettled me. They were her center, they glittered under smoked glass and reached out to me from within myself, like candle flames reflected in a window with nothing but pitch darkness beyond it.

Mills Loomis Mills

I had a hell of a time explaining all the soul resin stuff to Maya. I don't know if she thought I was crazy or high on metaphor or what. She wanted to be my girl-friend, though, she did say that, so I wasn't gonna hide anything from her. But I wasn't sure about being her boyfriend. The kind of business Mills is into makes it hard. A girl would hold you back.

She said, "So to become soul resin you have to curse God, and that'll do it?"

"If you bleed a lot," I explained.

"I don't see God being that way."

So naive. I said, "There may not be a God."

"Then how can *any* of that stuff happen?"

"It's not about God, it's about science. You know how they give people placebos—fake drugs—that are sup-posed to be wonderdrugs. And it works for 'em? Cures 'em? It may be something like that."

"What?" She hammered away. "What?"

"Everybody's gotta die. People have no control over it. But I think—and this is just a theory—that you do have some control on what happens to you afterward. But prob-ably it's just enough control to fuck it up somehow."

"So if you believe in God, but fuck up and bitch him out, then you're worse off than if you don't believe."

I snapped my fingers and pointed at her. "It's about the chemical make-up of the shed blood and how it metamorphoses after—that's what soul resin's about. Regular ghosts are different two ways: there's no blood factor at all. They're bloodless. That's why they're freer to roam around and pine, etcetera. But I think that also means they don't have much, y'know, consciousness."

"You mean they don't think and decide stuff?"

"They may be little more than zombies. I've gotten info drifting out of them before, but it's pretty patchy, pretty disorganized...pretty slim. The soul resin takes you there and shows you—where you can feel, smell, and everything—whole scenes. 'Cause of the blood."

Maya was sitting a yard or so from me on the back porch and the sun was coming up and starting to light up her face better. The look she had was like cautious, like somebody turning over a rock with a long stick to see if there are bugs or a snake under it.

I said, "Hear that whirring sound, like a table-saw way way off somewhere?"

She straightened up and did her head sideways like people trying to hear something faint even though it makes zero sense. "Yeah...I think so."

"Wanna go see what it is?"

"How would we find it?"

"I can find it."

"I bet it's that new condo thing they're building over on Bascomb."

(We were Uptown—heart of the beast).

I said, "Nope. Well, it could be there—not unlikely at all, actually. But it's not machinery."

She shrugged her shoulders sarcastically like she was saying you're the bigshot, what's the 411.

"It's somebody bleeding."

She wanted to laugh, started to, but believed too much of all the stuff I already told her to be able to. She said, "I don't wanna go see somebody bleeding. BUT—I don't think that's what it is, so sure, show me."

"You're not gonna freak out, right?"

"Depends on the amount of blood."

We cut out over the backyard fence and headed for it. I didn't know whether to be happy that I might end up with some help—which I majorly needed—or to worry that whatever the scene was that was waiting for us would be too much for the girl.

Jessamine Marie DuClous Bascomb

It was a Monday. I had not slept. Few had, for there was great suspense and trepidation in the air. The overwhelming torpor of the morning infected me as much with weakness as it filled others with a passion to smell gunpowder and singed flesh. Yet I appeared for the procession as I know all felt they must. Black, brown, yellow, and white, Creole and American, the Irish, the Germans, Italians. Catholic, Protestant, and Jew. Many had armed themselves.

I do not recall why, but I felt I should dress formally, though for daytime. I wore a gray *papeline* with a short jacket. Yet most opted to dress for a scrape, and wore looks that seemed better suited for night. The colored parade was headed by a stout boy of a *café au lait* complexion, who wore his yankee uniform and waved a large union flag. He was followed by a drum and fife corps. They played patriotic union airs, but in their characteristic country manner—for these must have been war migrants—disorderly and of less precise pitch than one would expect of more cultured players. Yet their manner of musicianing had always endowed me with a mood of devil-may-care frivolity. Therefore, as I was already happily drowsy from lack of sleep, I followed them, I daresay mildy entranced. Yes, white rowdies were also present, but I feared them not for they were, in the main, beardless youths. I must have been too faint to exercise my skills at, shall we call it, social arithmetic? I got a prompt lesson. One of the white youths—who appeared to me to be a gentleman's son—hurled a rock at a negro soldier and cursed him. He was quickly reprimanded by three black roustabouts who set upon him and began beating him. This was followed by a rush of white men who drew clubs and began thrashing the Negro offenders. A shot was fired. Then a volley. One of the white men emerged wounded, or so he acted. His face bellowed rage enough to steam his spectacles. He appeared to be a minor clerk, in collar and vest, and bare shirtsleeves, as if he had quit his shop in haste. There followed a generally senseless stampede of bodies, of varied and confused directions, I was roughly thrown into a wall where I stayed pinned.

they had me pinned against a wall it smelled like gas and we used to love the smell of gas 'cause it reminded us of road tripping

But as suddenly as the fracas began, it dispersed. Or the surging human mass which had spawned it simply had no time for it anymore, for it must continue lunging uptown. The black bodies, ringed on the sides by white, as a turbulent flood stream with foam on its banks, all continued in their meandering yet unflaggable thrust toward Canal Street and the Mechanic's Institute. Animosities had not subsided. Shots were no longer being fired and no blows traded, but of crude and injurious shouting there was plenty. It was either "Hang the rebels!" or "Kill the nigger yankee sons of bitches!" The presence of ladies quelled no one's vile language; indeed, the fairer sex—yes, myself included—joined in the rude verbal barrages. I feared not that some friend of my father's family would see me and report how low

I had sunk. So ardent was the general rehearsal for discord that no man noticed anyone save whom he might deem his mortal enemy.

Though after we had crossed Canal and entered the square before the Mechanic's Institute, a man did recognize me—from a great distance at that—and he appraised me with his eye as one would an enemy. And I a better friend than his business associates would ever be! It was Captain Clouet. From the second story window he eyed me with reproach and, I believe, fear. I wondered why he should fear me, with so many others calling for his execution in ringing and often eloquent tones. The procession was not able to get very far onto the square for the simple reason that it was already full with freedmen from other quarters of the city. Policemen were ranged on the periphery. One who I supposed must be a policeman sat astride his horse in full Confederate dress. I found his fashion out of season, and so did many of the colored men, particularly those wearing the Union blue. One of these shouted at the horseman, inquiring who he supposed had won the war, but the white man refused to countenance the question. He sat aloof, sporting the brutal and ugly smirk of those whose minds and hearts can never be swayed, no matter what force in the argument or compassion in the plea.

Clouet had retreated from the window, where I assume he had hoped to speak. He must have acknowledged what I had, but what, tragically, the unschooled freedmen apparently had not: the federal troops had failed to arrive. Or perhaps they had never intended to. It is quite possible that the invitation missed them, that they had not even heard there was to be a party—the channels for such information typically bypass the yankee's preferred bureaucratic roads. Possibly they had no knowledge of the primeval deity whose feast day had finally come, upon whose altar so many men that day burned.

November 22

Rafe Vidrine

Jessamine Bascomb was the daughter of Nash Newton Bascomb, a leading figure in the Crescent City White League. He probably engineered the short-lived coup that began in a pitched street battle at Liberty Place, 14 September, 1874. He had earlier helped to foment the 1866 riot. In the interviews I've had with her—which I now remember—she's talked at length about the political scene of the time. Had she lived today she probably would have some kind of career in, or commenting on, politics. But she's also not shy about airing sensitive laundry from her private life. She fluctuates strangely between a strict sense of social decorum and tirades full of pride, irreverence, and venom.

Her narrative style is in disarray, though. She talks about what she sees in front of her, often mixing it up with her century-old memories, and even lapses into sounding like a contemporary teeny-bopper druggie— maybe she's picked it up by listening?

My own life could come under a similar heading, disarray. Because the question of the rational feasibility of my and Jessamine Bascomb's relationship is so daunting, I've chosen not to question it at all. I feel like the schizoid who sees some ugly demon out of the corner of his eye and opts to fix the problem by not looking out of the corner of his eye anymore. Except in my case, what I see is directly in front of me, and a demon she's not. More like an animated John Singer Sargeant portrait, in celluloid. Long, elegant. Like penmanship used to be.

But she has a strange effect on me, which I doubt is healthy. She's dead. I'm interacting with death. Isn't that bound to have adverse consequences? The contrary seems to be the case. I feel twenty years younger. I feel vigorous, even though I can't even move when she's in front of me. I get woozy. I cry. I hate myself. I think I hate myself because I can't help admiring her.

But all she is, really, is just a trick of light. She *is* gone. So why is she still here? I feel monumentally unequipped to address these new questions. Of course I do already know so much about her, really. Her father, anyway. All out of books, though, and reading doesn't prepare one adequately for seeing.

Another surprise is that she seems every bit as dumbfounded as me about the fact of our communication. She said something like, "Had I known how brute force of concentrated will could alter the intended channels of God's dominions with such success, I would certainly have applied with alacrity to the circumvention of my death in the first place!"

Well, I'm exaggerating, but it does tend in that direction. Whatever it was, she laughed when she said it. It was a joke! *She laughs!* It was really more like a decorous, flirty chuckle.

She says, though, that she has a pressing cause behind this exertion of her allegedly dead will. Mills Loomis Mills. His name stood out as the one thing that was not a surprise. She said he's conceived a plot that could radically alter the age-old relations between dead and living.

Also, she thinks I got him started on it somehow. She knows I was his teacher once, but she also knows I'm black so she probably thinks I was his hoodoo teacher. But not even Dr. John and Marie Laveau together could cook up this stuff: the souls of certain dead people, Jessamine Bascomb says, distill down into a brackish viscous resin. The experience of these souls is said to be one of— what was it?—"direst agony?" But she couldn't or wouldn't elaborate as to who ends up in such a state.

This kind of thing is really more Mattie LaVonne's department—cross-cultural images of embodied evil, hell, etc. I'm sure there's some old Indian tale that has it, as well as from ancient Greece and everywhere else. But I haven't studied that line one whit. I always thought it was real people and their actions—I mean while alive— that mattered. I mean, a historical figure is not the bones in the coffin somewhere, but the figure that's presented in the people's memory, right? I always remembered what Mother Jones said, "Pray for the dead and fight like hell for the living." Now I don't know what to do.

Then she asked about Lucius Holt. Him again. I said, "Lady, you get around," but whenever I try to play with her, she doesn't seem to get it. So I answered her question and said he was just an obscure kid who was apparently murdered, though no one ever found out by whom. And that, way back in the '40s. 1940s, that is. Then she asked a question that threw me more than everything else, even though I can't see why it would in retrospect: "Was a great deal of blood let in the incident?"

Dear Mills,

Well, we just took off and there's this gross old guy sitting next to me who keeps asking everything I'm doing. I told him I'm writing a suicide note and I'm taking everybody else in the plane down with me. Not really. If you were here, I would have, though, and we would've both been laughing now.

I know I just saw you fifteen minutes ago, but still I feel like I miss you already. I think I know what you mean now about how it's probably not a smart idea to be in love because of how it makes you dependent on somebody. Like I should be all psyched about going out to New Mexico and doing archaeology out there, but I've gotta worry about missing you instead. And like you always say, everybody walks through the exit door alone. You're so morbid. I guess you're right, though. But maybe it's not so bad to just not think about it.

This guy keeps looking over at my letter. I hope he reads this—I'VE GOT A BOMB IN MY CARRY-ON THAT MY CRAZY BOYFRIEND GAVE ME!

WE'RE ALL GOING DOWN!

I feel like making a long check-list for you about everything to do while I'm gone, but that would be too mom-like. There's just one thing. I really do hope you're gonna write me, but I have this feeling you're not. You'll get this even before I get out to the reservation, I bet. Wouldn't it be cool if there was something from you already waiting for me when I get out there? Then I'll have to eat my words. (But I'd rather be eating you-you can send me a dirty letter if you want)

Uh-oh, I bet this dirty old GROSS man is getting a thrill now. No one to protect me! You'll have to come out to the desert later and beat off all the beasts and savages for me. And then I'll owe you-"Whatever you want" (I know you love to hear me say that)

Oh, well, in love and lust,
April Mae Mills-Toy

Jessamine Marie DuClous Bascomb

At what a gruesome scene our Mills Loomis Mills now officiates! And he seems to have won for himself a confederate. A fair-faced girl of a few years his junior. She watches as Mills leans over the dying man and touches and smells his unstaunched blood. The sun peeks round, through the quiet early spaces between trees and houses, thus slowly illuminating what no one should see, whether that one be simply shade, as I, or living body. But the despoiler is not aware that the police are en route. They will surely thwart his efforts at least in the short term, though I fear his plan will ring too fantastic to cause them to fear for their resting loved ones over here.

He must indeed be a policeman, for he wears the standard upon his lapel. Yet he, too, bloodies his knife, thrusting it in turn with the others. Their victim recently leapt from the second story and had attempted to flee, only he must have injured himself in landing upon the ground, for his running was hampered and he was quickly treed. They commenced the stabbing immediately. His cries soon became groans. I ceased hearing him just as smoke and powder stung the eyes and blurred the witnessing.

*first you feel it and then it stops, it's not pain any-
more it's just you feel dull tickling like inside you and
you don't know what's going on 'cause you don't want
to look and see that they're stabbing you my dream is
that a bunch of people are shooting at each other and
beating each other up it looks like Europe except there's
black people everywhere and they don't have them
much do they?*

You must intercede. He draws nearer and nearer to
realization of his reckless aim. But he will first have to
learn that the only blood which will awaken the sleeping resin is that from a living body freshly spilt. His
clumsy efforts to make use of the blood of this poor
bleeder lying wounded in the overtrod city grass will
prove fruitless. He must kill, and do it right over the
feckless brooding memory of Lucius Holt: then only will
the explosive contact between then and now send him
hurtling to the fabulous imagined "New Mexico" he
seeks—or suck him under—and then all of *us* may be lost.

*Mills? Did I oversleep? I had this like long dream, like
a whole life and in the end you were playing with this dead
guy, it was gory*

Clouet once more at the window? Or have they
got him? No, he's just a memory. And now not a pleasant one anymore, at that. When was it he grew the
shadow on his brow and began to cultivate contempt for
me? Though once he had been attentive with his cares,
he became quite cool, aloof, and finally brutal. One
evening he was in a particularly ill humor. I suspect he
had been at the Mechanic's Hall learning afresh of the
political impasse he increasingly found himself in. They
beat him horribly and would have hanged him, had he
not changed into a porter's uniform before fleeing the
structure. But he got his new constitution, and society
changed such that we could dare be seen in the various
public conveyances and entertainment places together—

not arm in arm, of course, but together. Indeed, arm-in-arm it was in many a narrow passage of the Creole districts. For there I resided—with him, in fact. He explained that a cohabitation of our peculiar kind was not at all unusual in his neighborhood, had never been. My mother had already led me to believe as much. Though, sadly, after the war she denied ever having intimated such a thing, implied instead that the Frenchmen of Louisiana, in a quite contrary fashion to Frenchmen everywhere else, had limited their romantic attentions to a select color of woman only. However, regarding Captain Clouet, I sensed that he had always been loath to house me under his roof. For my own part, the displeasure I seemed to invoke in him only goaded me on, for I disliked his common habit of growling in low-pitched undertones without petitioning me directly as to whatever his point of contention may have been. I was enjoying a footbath, for I had been all day afoot in the *Vieux Carré* observing social developments grand and small along the public ways—this was my favorite pastime then, and now my only one. The Italians had come and added their fruit-laden carts to the crush about the *Place d'Armes*. I delighted in hearing their *patois* and mingling it with the others, the Parisian and Louisiana French, the Irishman's fiery and American's bland English, which roots could be heard in the strange, complex consonants of the German brickmasons. Out of this bustle of exotic and familiar shouts and murmurs I would pass upward, to the *allée* of willows crowning the levee, and from there view cathedral, Cabildo and Presbytere, market, plaza, and balconied Pontalbas all in a single majestic sweep. Only the statue of Jackson at the center of the square's radiating walks and gardens perturbed me. I knew not yet what omen it betook.

It was not General Jackson, however, who entered my rooms that same evening without a knock and proceeded to the sideboard without even the most perfunctory greeting. It was one lesser in rank, a Captain only—and that bolstered by doubtful military accomplishment—Clouet. I had taken note of late that he seemed reluctant to wait on me in even the most innocuous of attentions. I resolved to press the matter in the hope that it might bay his beast, bring it out into the open light so that I might learn its nature. In married couples, such a womanly ploy is called nettling, but ours was not an orthodox union. I asked if he might not pour me a madeira, and announced that I felt faint. I got no reply. He ignored me. I observed the back of his head tip back and heard the report of his emptied glass striking the marble inlay of the sideboard. I emboldened myself to press him further, "Captain Clouet, *ma foi!*" I cried. "Do you think it unusual that an apartment might be occupied by its inhabitant, and that she might rightfully expect a bit of courtesy as payment for entry?"

At this he turned his rage not upon me, but upon the girl who attended to my feet, the poor Clothilde. "Clothilde!" he shouted, as I observed the rare and peculiar red that sometimes suffused his golden face, "have you not heard mam'sell's request?" Clothilde rose and bowed her head and stood sheepishly before him, and it shamed me to see her made to cower there. "Miss Bascomb hails from one of the finest families of the second municipality!"—this said with a jocular sneer—"The American quarter's charms have failed to secure Miss Bascomb's enduring interest, yet the level of service she grew accustomed to there must not be spared her here."

He then turned and filled his glass once more as I bade Clothilde go. I reclined and smiled—this I had always been taught well to do—and waited some moments before saying, "I had no idea in what low esteem you held your own pedigree."

*he's got a couple of champions in it, 'Shoba, he's
our dog. He's a yellow lab but he's real red looking so
we called him "Neshoba" 'cause that's Choctaw for
"wolf" and we got him in Mississippi but we didn't get
him from Neshoba county we got him from around
Natchez 'cause me and Mills go up there a lot it's so
romantic and there's good places to canoe and Mills'
uncle has a place out in the woods around there that's
a great place to get away but Mills gets weird sometimes around old things, like buildings or whatever,
like in Natchez and New Orleans, too, trippy like he's
listening for something all the time like a twig snap-
ping behind him, in Vicksburg he got really weird one
time and sat down out in the middle of one of those
battlefield cemeteries with all the little unmarked head-
stones, and sat down and acted like he was meditating
and wouldn't talk to me*

I have been often to Natchez. Father had always
dreamed of marrying me off to some Stanton or
Dunleith or O'Whatagain up there. He knew well my
probable value. Ah, *maman*, what a price he paid for
your French flesh! And not just at the act of sale. Once
I accompanied Clouet—by steamer?—to the Grande
Dame on the bluffs. As I recall, Clouet pressed on.
Yes, he had a political meeting at Jefferson Bend. But
travel together we did, and often. I suppose everything was in such a speedy whirlwind then, though
only for a short time I fear, that one could do almost
anything without an upbraiding, or worse. We reclined across from each other, the oaks of Feliciana
rushed by. Perhaps we were in a rail car, or perhaps
horse-drawn. I remarked that he seemed to be passing much more time of late among the American Negroes, rather than among his own people. He replied
to the effect that his people had grown mistrustful of
him, and added, "'Pragmatic' is an American word.

147

We French generally tend more towards firebrands, if not simply towards *beurre noir* and brandy."

"*Eh bien,* a dinner invitation! This is language a woman understands."

"Ha, ha"—his smile was precious, it affected one like glinting jewelry—"*mais,* you are not that kind of woman, mam'sell. Though woman you certainly are."

His flattery only drove me on, in fact, it was designed to do so. He sought many occasions to solicit my counsel on such "men's" matters. "The *Black Republican* has it that you and your ilk are an arrogant, dissolute, and, well, un-American lot of depraved Gallic sots."

"Yes," sighed he, "and this notion is precisely why we cannot rely on them. They look to the north, where, in most cases, they may not vote and are severely restricted in many matters of law. They err in the view that the Anglo-Saxons of New York and Illinois feel themselves to be any less their masters than the Anglo-Saxons of Red River."

"Ah, but they perceive also that many of their masters were French, and colored, you Creoles."

"This they overemphasize."

"Overemphasize? Your rhetoric is perhaps more subtle than they appreciate. The American is not fond of such delicate distinction, he prefers something to be set down in round numbers."

"We made the numbers clear enough, in '67. Unlimited male suffrage. This number they heeded, though General Banks and his Yankees opposed us."

"As I did, as well. I found your number one half the desirable size. Indeed, my own recollection has it that you, too, opposed this round number, that you found it too large, in fact."

"A miscalculation which cost me no American friends, white or black. The illiterate American Negroes did not seem to resent that the illiterate be restricted from voting. It was my literate and cultured dear friends who hated me for suggesting it."

"And why did you cease looking to Paris, to 1789, to 1848, why do you now sing of 1776?"

"*C'est la bête politique*," he replied, raising his flask.

I have difficulty seeing you, but I know you are there for I can hear your breathing. It sounds labored— I hope you are not unwell. As for seeing, it's simply a matter of waiting. Sometimes I see you clearly. Yet soon enough the living world becomes distracted from me and drifts away. I am sure there are a host of reasons as well, for...everything. There are a host of *us*. Bethink yourself of a great and dense, clinging fog. That is what it is like to see through my eyes. And Professor, the fog is us. We are not solidly constructed. We drift about like disparate flotsam in the air, yet the air, too, is us. Merely to remember enough to contain oneself as an individual is an arduous struggle—and there are long sleeps, when one forgets altogether who one is.

None of us has any privacy. The new girl is lucky. She knows not yet where she has arrived. Ah, there you are!

Love it was not, never. Though *amour*, perhaps. Pleasure it was, briefly. But then he was suddenly like a poorly aged wine, gone vinegar. Whichever came first— his new rudeness or my new distaste for him—our close living arrangement soon became impossible. On a Sunday morning after a party in his home, because I remained steadfast in my refusal to bed with him, he burst into my quarters in a great rage. Then he softened his demeanor and fell upon his knees at my bedside and begged me to grant him some little intimacy. But I remained unaffected. He then rose and assumed an air of quiet finality: "You do me no good. Already rumors of your residence here harm my interests. And now I pay a price against receipt of nothing. Not companionship. Not service. Not consideration. Yet turn you out I cannot bring myself to do."

Indeed, he would not. Yet his resentment grew, he nourished it on visits to my rooms at inappropriate hours, and on increasingly crude statements spoken in my presence. His final lapse of tact came in the wake of heavy cloying rains and fever.

The yellow fever? Was I stricken? Was he? Back of his plot were rows upon rows of crude, unarchitectural frame structures, some built literally over infested ponds, and beyond that the morass of a great city's refuse—upon every riverbound wind death's stench rallied. And then there were better days. At any rate, many across the city spent their first flush of renewed good health at the interments of loved ones. My mother's passing occured around one of the more trying times. I don't recall whether I attended the funeral. I only know I have never seen her since. When Clouet came to me on the patio where I sought to recuperate from whatever calamity it was that had recently rocked me, he spoke softly but insolently, insinuating demands. When I bade him leave me in peace he raised his hand in a violent attitude. When he aborted the gesture, I spoke firmly to him. "No man has ever yet struck me, not even my putrid kaintock cracker father who has the greatest right. He who enjoys the privilege of being the first shall not live a long and boastful life."

His audacity, however, was not to be quelled. He spoke in grave tones of his influence among the Negro Militia. And as if his base threat could not suffice, he then laughed and groped at my hair, like a jungle ape attempting a human trick. I was incensed, and I apprised him of it. What maddened me was his blind devotion to a vision of his own magnitude which fell so at odds with the reality of his predicament, with me, and with society at large. I sought to remind him of things he should not have been so naive as not to know. "Captain, you live in the past. The Creole districts have no more autonomy. Spoons Butler put an end to that. He also saw to it that there would be no more French in the schools. You are no longer a Frenchman, Captain, or a Creole, you are a Negro. The Yankees have worked it out as well as my father did, in the years before the war. You must understand, *mon capitaine*, that if the transgressor who wrongs me happens to be a Negro—be he octoroon or nigger-black—the price of the assassin will be cheaper. And your uniformed men, they will not survive long in the livery you have bestowed upon them, not in our locale."

I didn't survive, Mills, I didn't survive.

Rafe Vidrine

On November 23, 1876, Alphonse Clouet was hanged for the murder of Jessamine Bascomb.

But somehow I don't think he did it. I finally worked up the nerve to ask her about it, but she claimed she didn't remember. Which I don't believe either. Do ghosts lie? If so, why would they?

I've been busier in the two days since my first sighting of Miss Bascomb (Nov. 13) than I've been in quite a few years. I had been experiencing something like apathy, especially in regard to my work. My mind had always flown off to Lauren, or Mills Loomis Mills, or to sleep. Most importantly, I had stopped believing in the point of historical research, verification, disputation. No, not the grand scale of it, but as far as the microscopic details, I really stopped being sure they counted for anything at all. But now one of these small details has come vividly to…if not life, animation. I guess all the pep-talks and shame-talks to students over the years never convinced me in my gut what I kept telling them: these people "back then," they were real people. Then they died and became something different.

So this real woman, who is now dead, has com-missioned me to track down and verify a small con-temporary detail—Mills Loomis Mills, who means to become a big detail before his time is up.

I've shared some of this with Mattie, but out of some knee-jerk skepticism that inserts itself on the way from my mind to my mouth, I've left doors open for metaphysical or psychological interpretations. Mattie has opted for a theological reading (Indian-style, of course). She doesn't like the implications of it. She thinks either that the screen between this world and the "upper" one is thinning for me, which means im-pending death, or that Miss Bascomb is some guide who is intended to prepare me for the same event. Doesn't look like too bright a future, whichever one. But it's my own fault that she's off track like this, be-cause I don't—not since my first flabbergasted vision—name names. I describe images, imply stories, indi-cate that a form of dialogue is taking place. But Mattie doesn't know that my apparition friend has a name, a birth-date, a death certificate (listing cause of death, even). Or that she took another life down with her, after she went herself.

All this means I have to keep Mattie in the dark more and more, because she's been pretty imperative that I resist communication with this "spirit" as she calls it, says she's not ready for me to go yet. Well, I guess my new friend is a "spirit." But she doesn't seem like what I thought that word meant. So I find myself distracted and lying when I'm with Mattie, which, of course, makes me want to be around her less. She seems pretty hurt by the whole mess. First woman I hurt that way in probably thirty years. Maybe that's another reason I feel young again suddenly.

What I've been busy with is trying to discover Mills, not anymore out of a vague itching obsession,

but as an assignment. He's a hard one to locate. I
contacted his family but wasn't surprised to hear they
haven't heard from him. They asked me what he was
up to these days. I said I didn't know. I'm learning to
lie at a late age—after getting used to, it's not so bad.
It was his mother I talked to. Guess daddy "done run
off." There's a theory of greatness for you, the ones
from what they used to call "broken homes" always
have something to prove. Including Rafe Vidrine? Rafe
doesn't recall much from childhood. Just the facts,
which mostly happened to other people.

In our telephone conversation, Tammy (what she
asked me to call her) expounded widely, if disjoint-
edly, on the theme of her loss of a son. She called him
Loomis. Said something happened to that boy along
the way. Chapter one covers his sweet-natured, grinning toddlerhood through East Baton Rouge High, nice
girls, football (on the team but never played, "except
maybe but once"). Then comes chapter two: mari-
juana and a little hippie girlfriend, both of which ru-
ined him and turned him against his family—which
Tammy said was the absolute ruin of everybody. There
was a baby crying, and she put the phone down more
than once to hiss reprimands at it. She asked me if I
was close with my family. I dodged the question, but
it's been dogging me ever since.

Will I see them again? Recognize them? Is there a
black belt over there with some ground-zero intersec-
tion where everybody knows everybody? No, there's
bound to be too many of them. Miss Bascomb makes
it sound like the whole world is a close and crowded
tenement. But whatever the congregation is over there,
Lucius Holt's not in it. Miss Bascomb says he isn't like
the others; soul resin is different. It can't move. Not in
space, time, or memory. It can't see. It doesn't know
where it is and never learns. It's a thirty-second record

of a soul trapped in death-pangs, "scorched black," Miss Bascomb says, "as by a thunderbolt hurled from above."

No wonder Mills is interested. Right up his alley. When I talked to his mother I kept picturing him as a boy pulling legs off a bug and watching for little six-eyed facial expressions. Wanting to see into death is understandable and human, but not like this boy is into it. I never thought I would use this word, but Mill's ambition seems "unwholesome."

But I know something Miss Bascomb doesn't, and I've tried to tell her, and that's something about the character of this boy. I doubt he's capable. I know the type because I've seen them come in and out of school for, well, decades. They don't finish, ever. They change majors five times, get within two credits of graduating, then run off to another new ridiculous life-plan, never dotting one i or crossing one t. I think Mills is like this. No stick-to-it-ness.

Also, where will he get the blood Jessamine Bascomb says he'll need? Cut himself? *Kill* somebody? Or just kindly request them to bleed a few pints worth? He'd have to have some kind of mighty motivation to work up the energy for any of those options. I'm curious, though, let's say "intrigued" about all of it.

The other mystery has to do with me. It's the primary reason for my new sense of youthfulness. I actually feel physically younger, more vital, since I've been in contact with the dead. And this feeling is grounded in real physical developments. My eyesight, for example. It's been clearing up. A miracle. Vague shapes have grown back their sharp outlines. It's what I imagine stem-cell therapy to be like. Like a dehydrated creature filling up slowly with water, a green muscularity is spreading through me. Do I thank Jessamine for this? Do I thank death? Or life? Maybe life and death are like yin and yang, maybe the contrast makes each stronger. I wish I could shout all this to Mattie. Tell her I can see her. I just want to tell her I think she's pretty.

Mills Loomis Mills

Maya freaked all right, no doubt. I got a little freaked too, though, 'cause the guy wasn't all the way dead yet. It was at the construction site where we thought it was at, on Bascomb, but it would've been easy to find anyway 'cause when we were still a few blocks away the sound of the blood got suddenly louder and higher—another wound. The crime was obviously still in progress, so I wanted to be real careful approaching the place, but Maya was being all fun and silly about it and made lots of noise skipping across the street to the site, and I almost let her just run into it alone 'cause maybe that's what somebody gets for not taking somebody seriously. I couldn't though. I ran after her and kept up with her and saw her leap up onto this stack of cinderblocks and then she jumped right back down and came whispering at me about how we needed to get out of there. All crazy-scared looking. So I told her to chill, and I went and checked it out. The dude appeared to be belly-shot, but that couldn't have been the first little pinging that we heard. It must've been when we heard the big acceleration— because that's what it sounds like, it's like a blender and first it was on grate and then it got bumped up to puree: when the victim got shot a second time. The first time was probably just a scrape or something. Turns out Maya's antics probably scared off the shooter—well, stabber more likely—'cause he didn't seem to be anywhere around (lucky for us, lucky for *her*, I told her). Probably just your everyday assailant killing for money or pride. Why even bother to number them?

The victim looked up at me, but I couldn't tell if he was seeing me or not. His hands were on his gut like he was trying to hold something in there. I couldn't just leave him after he looked at me, though. Black guy. Had a tattoo on his chest: "The World Is Mine." I wondered if Lucius Holt's eyes looked like that before he finally bit it. Then I started to wonder, honestly, if it was respectful to fuck with Holt's soul remnants at all. But that's the thing about conscience making cowards out of everybody. That's why Hamlet never did shit, really, and what sets somebody like Jesus apart, he didn't want to go through with it, but he did anyway. What Jesus was was a great Scientist, and that eating of body and drinking of blood worked for centuries before they forgot how to do it.

I told Maya to go call 911. She said, "Are you sure?"

I said, "Yeah, big deal, just do it." There was a payphone right there by this bar on the corner—bar was closed, looked like, or private party. Nobody was around to see her do it, use a phone to save a guy's life. Some people are so worried a cop's gonna bust them for drugs that they'd just as soon never call them for anything. It was that time of day when the birds make the big ruckus before the sun comes and puts them back to sleep again. I said, "It's the right thing to do, anyway, why would you worry about it?"

She said, "I dunno." She ran off to do it (she runs everywhere, that's the way she is), but I said wait and got her bag of weed off her. She said "Good idea" like I was saving her from the cops (paranoid stoning tripping shit), but really I wanted the baggie to see if I could get some of the blood in it somehow.

I went back to the guy, but he seemed to be slipping. Didn't seem to know I was there, but his eyes were still open and moving around. The blood started to sound like a wheezing chorus in a giant emphysema ward. And after hearing the old stuff, the fresh sounds just didn't flip my skirt anymore. I told the guy it was gonna be OK and we had an ambulance on the way.

It was frustrating trying to get blood off him though. Try it with water: pouring a glass of water into a baggie is pretty easy, but if the water's spilt, it's hard, and, like the saying says, blood is thicker than water. I tried squeezing the guy's soaked-up shirt out—he'd taken it off and bunched it up around the wound—but it didn't work too well. Pretty impossible.

The guy didn't care what I was doing, he was just glad I was there. He probably figured I was doing some medical thing.

Maya came back and was standing on the stack of cinderblocks looking at me funny. Finally the only thing I could think of was I took off my shoes and then my socks (and wished for just once they weren't all crusty) and let them soak up a bunch of the stuff coming out of him and just crammed them into the baggie. Why, I don't know. Stupid.

Maya wanted to git before the cops came—like I should have, the way they hate me—but the guy actually gripped me with his bloody hand. My hands were pretty bloody too by now—and no way to use it! He looked at me like "man, don't go don't leave me to die alone," but I said, "S'alright, s'alright." But I was going.

But I couldn't. I couldn't bring myself to get upright and walk. Run off.

Then Maya hops down next to me and grabs my other arm hard and points. First I couldn't tell at what. The half-built condo cinderblock ugliness or the shells and mud and sand it stuck up out of? She stopped pointing but still was looking over there. There was a couple of two-by-fours and loose bricks on the ground, so I thought for one little second, well, she *is* a Deadhead, maybe she wants to make bookcases out of them, but why think of that at a time like this?

Then she says, "Is that her?"

April Brunnen

What are you doing and who's that girl? It looks like New Orleans around here, like Uptown. Remember that one trip we had it was in Audubon Park and we had to hide and keep down from the cops cruising around shining their lights across the lagoon? And before morning these weird looking strips of fog went walking across the golf course and we said they looked like ghosts. That was fun, but this is kind of creepy. I know I'm probably still in New Mexico so I'm just dreaming about you. But you're just in my dream, you're not part of it, I can tell 'cause of how you're ignoring me. You're like in a movie. So I guess that girl's probably supposed to be me, too, I know that's how dreams work sometimes. This one flips around a lot this lady's here watching it with me. She talks like she's out of a book except in New Mexico, sometimes it's back there and she's not around then and that's the nightmare part. It was like a rape dream, but it wasn't like the dreamy way it usually is in dreams, where you don't really feel it they cut me and stuff too. I found out in Psych that was called a mutilation dream, but I forgot what it was supposed to mean.

There was a time when the name of Clouet stayed happily absent from my thoughts. Until one day, afternoon, evening, after a rain had cooled the breezes and sent the shadows slanting into my rooms on Customhouse Street, soaking all in a gray stillness, she came, Clara Reina Clouet. She had come to meet me of her own accord, announcing something about the magnetic force of my notoriety. I offered coffee, but she expressed a preference for wine. So I replied that it was a preference I shared, and we proceeded to indulge liberally. She had recently returned from France, and I, perceiving her bold stare but daring not interpret it, asked in wonder why visiting with me should be such a pressing order of business so soon after her homecoming. She answered, in measured tones and all asmirk, "Assuming I have not been misinformed by my brother's vituperations, I have every reason to believe that you are quite an exceptional woman. One I thought I should very much like to meet."

"You embarrass me," I protested. Yet I could already tell that our new acquaintance would bear fruit in the form of many happy hours flying from the despot Tedium, so I assented to her offer of friendship with a smile and a touch. A touch! Indeed, more than a touch, for I grasped her wrist with the resolute but gentle force her brother had once applied to me, and she responded with the same look of dizziness and loss which once must have descended upon my own face.

He started right when I first got here with these weird touches that were supposed to be all crunchy and down-homey, but I could tell even then that he was a pervert that wanted to do his daughter or his niece and I looked like her so he undressed me with his eyes whenever I wasn't looking. Mr. Bigshot Anthropologist with everything to lose. I dreamed I lived in New Mexico out in the middle of nowhere on this flat red dust floor between ridges of mesa. On this reservation and I was learning Navajo and the Indians I met were mostly really cool but distant to me so I hung out with the other Americans—whites, I guess but there was a black guy and he's more like a white guy to them because he's just not one of them, I'm not one of them either, and God knows Dr. Schlacht ain't but he married one, so he's kind of hononary. Honorary guy all around except he should have his dick cut off and bleed to death in a cage hanging from a pole in the sun dripping on everybody like him but he never will. But I also dreamed I was with you and now I'm dreaming like that because I can see you but now the police have got you and you're ignoring me again. Yeah, fuck you. You used to call these kind of dreams the epic dreams and said they were the best but sometimes they just go on and on and you get sick of them it's making me dizzy I feel sick. But in a way I don't feel anything.

He can't hear you, child.

Shut up, I don't even know who you are

So rude!

I can do anything I want in my own dream, nobody'll ever know. Mills said that's what you should do, break all the rules and do whatever outrageous things you can think of 'cause it's the only time you'll get away with it. Like he does, too, like he was digging around in this big fat black dead guy a second ago, or maybe not dead, maybe just dream dead like when somebody's definitely dead but then the next second they're up smiling and walking around and stuff and none of it's a surprise. Anyway, I have no idea what the dead or just resting black guy's supposed to mean. Mills? Now you're not even here? I've been through a lot, fuck you! Fuck you, man, you're being a shit.

Rafe Vidrine, from Beyond Yellow and Black: Franco-African Political Culture in Louisiana

Alphonse Clouet was unusual among the black creole leadership in that he was the offspring of a *plaçage*, a peculiar but not uncommon kind of liaison in antebellum New Orleans between a wealthy (usually white) gentleman, and his quadroon or octoroon mistress. The tradition originated among the French-speaking Creoles downtown, but it soon took root uptown as well, to the chagrin of many an Anglo-Saxon wife. Long and often demanding courtships preceded consummation in many such cases. Aside from the social status he was able to attain, the story of Clouet's parentage was not atypical.

Like many of his contemporaries, Rodolphe Clouet met his future mistress at a quadroon ball, sometime in 1826. A yearlong courtship followed during which he got to know the fifteen year-old Olympe Suarez and her family. Oscar Suarez, the girl's father, had earned his freedom through service in the Spanish colonial militia, and his Frenchmen Street tailoring business was successful enough by 1811 to purchase two slaves. One of these would give birth to Alphonse Clouet's mother. Like many of his generation and class, he was a joiner,

a founding member of two of antebellum New Orleans' most important black fraternal societies: *La
Société Catholique pour l'Instruction des Orphelins dans
l'Indigence*, and the *Benevolent Association of the Veterans of 1815*. Alphonse Clouet would later capitalize
on his grandfather's membership in the latter organi-
zation, using its prestige to help recruit other free
negroes, first for the Confederacy, then for the Union
armies.

There is reason to believe that Suarez may have
solicited Rodolphe Clouet's interest in his daughter. Both
men had served in the defense of New Orleans against
the British in 1815, and Suarez later claimed he had originally made Clouet's acquaintance on the Chalmette
battlefield. In a letter of July 1850, Suarez wrote, "How
sensible it seemed to me that comrades in arms would
get on well also in the more peaceable pursuits of
trade and family." It also seems clear that Suarez considered the infusion of white blood into his descendants' bloodline a wise and good thing. If Olympe
Suarez' diaries are to be trusted, she, too, held high
esteem for European bloodlines. Her writing on racial
subjects is scant but clear: she had a disdain for black-
ness and hoped for her descendants to become whiter
and whiter throughout the generations. Since these
kinds of views were rather anomalous in the free colored community of Creole New Orleans, it may be
that they account for Alphonse Clouet's later ability to
conform more quickly than his contemporaries to
American models of race relations and racial identity.

At any rate, the *plaçage* was formalized in 1827
and Olympe Suarez gave birth first to a daughter, and
then to Alphonse, March 29, 1830. Although Rodolphe
Clouet was also married, and never legally severed
ties with his white wife—he continued to make his
home with her until his death in 1855—they never

had children. It may be because of this that the elder Clouet cultivated close and affectionate bonds with his children by Olympe Suarez. The *plaçage* agreement called for a set amount of money to be allocated yearly, and stipulated modest provisions for the children's education. But Clouet went beyond his contractual obligations, spending time with the children and eventually paying for both to be educated in Paris.

It was in Paris that the young Alphonse made the acquaintance of Jean-Charles Houzeau, and it would be Clouet who would later convince the Belgian astronomer and editor that his Radical political vision could best be realized in Reconstruction New Orleans. Their correspondence during the 1850s reveals the voracious rate at which Clouet absorbed—and disposed of—new political ideas. It was fortuitous for Clouet's political development that he arrived in Europe in the summer of 1848, and much of the discussion in the Clouet-Houzeau letters centers around the revolutionary aspirations and failures of that turbulent year. It was during the subsequent decade that Clouet developed his peculiar brand of racialist syndicalism, more akin to the black separatism of African colonization societies than to the color-blind integrationism of the radical Creoles. However, this turn would arise out of bitter defeat, cynicism, and despair. The young Clouet came nearer to a kind of miscegenationist ideal. In a letter of 1851, after predicting that the Compromise of 1850 would precipitate rather than delay open war between the sections, Clouet wrote:

> Many have despaired over the role of nationalism in the liberation of the people. The fugitive Germans denounce it while their brethren at Frankfort [sic] debate only its scope, not its desirability. The question before their assembly became not "Should there be a

Germany?" but rather "How large will Germany be?"
In France, M. Prudhon has wisely realized that *vive la
France!* inflames his Parisian rabble with far greater
success than *vive la liberte!* However, as tempestu-
ously as these questions seem to grip and rattle Europe, it is in the United States of America—which, I
must add, will not remain so long—that the question
of nationality will drive men to the severest test of
their wits and determination. For while the Constitution speaks only of "Americans," what the "American"
sees on the streets of his new cities and on the num-
berless rural ways are Germans, Scots, Irishmen,
Frenchmen, and the masses of those whose purpose
in the history of the people remains yet to be defined:
the Africans. This state of affairs would seem already
to present the most intractable of difficulties, yet
America nurses also many varieties of mongrels, exotic and heretofore unknown to man. What role will
these children of divers fathers expect to play in the
majestic shaping of the future of a country who knows
not nationhood? They will be the heralds of the new
era, mitigating passions ignoble and just, distributing
the spoils of toppled tyrannies among the quarreling
tribes, to each her due: if only God grant requisite
pluck and fortitude to them who would lead![5]

It is clear as early as this letter that Clouet intended
to summon the "requisite pluck and fortitude" for himself. The death of his father would provide him with his
first move in the delicate game of racial intercession that
would be the hallmark of his political style.

Mills Loomis Mills

They finally hauled me in. Screamed homicide in my face. Said it wasn't playing around time anymore. I agreed but they didn't know why.

I don't know what happened with Maya. Guess she booked in time. I looked up to where she was at and there was a blue-clad porker instead. They say in France the cops are slim and pretty. That makes France the only nation on earth of its kind. The one that busted me was a typical fat wop-looking one. He came around the stack of cinder-blocks like Baretta and Kojak and Don Johnson all rolled into one and demoted back to uniform and pissed because of that, shouting at me to stand up slowly and step away from the body. I said, "He's not a body yet, he's still breathing." I backed up a little bit and another one came from behind and tackled me. Slammed me onto the ground and rode on me there like he was making bacon with his skinny beaten-up wife, feeling me up, cuffing me with those new plastic ribbon things. It took a little while longer for the EMTs to show, 'cause you know they got their priorities: bust people first, then try to save some sucker's life. The cops looked pretty unstoked when the ambulance pulled up, they looked at each other like, "Damn, if the nigger makes it, we won't be able to put the freak away."

Yeah, sure, I told them about me being the one to show up and call 911. First they told me to shut up. Like that pumped way they do it, "SHUT UP I SAID SHUT UP," spit flying, regulation moustaches jumping off their faces. Then the sergeant showed up and he was black so he was nicer. But just because I'm lucky and white, I hear the black ones are just as bad as white when it's black busting black. I'm right 'cause then I watched the black sergeant (well, he was yella, actually) whispering some vicious thing into the victim's ear. They had him up on the stretcher and they were moving him into the ambulance and the sergeant made them stop and smiled in a mean way at the almost dead suffering guy until he realized he wasn't getting noticed and that's when he said whatever he did in his ear. The victim shook his head and moaned like a kid that just got a bad report card and knew his pa was gonna whip him, "Naw, naw." Then they put him in the ambulance and the sergeant shouted at him, "Don't git too comfortable now, we'll be seein' y'soon." Guess they had something on him.

They wanted something on me, too, so they ran my name through their anti-human internet spiderweb *Machine* but I won—'cause I didn't give them my real name. See, I know that even though I've never been booked for anything, they got special files for folks they don't like. I told them my name was Rodolphe Desdunes. He's been dead too long for them to have dirt on him. But you know, cops have a heightened sense of smell, like dogs, they can smell guilt, just too often it's the wrong kind.

They didn't like the blood on my hands. They said so, one of 'em said, "I don't like all that blood on his hands," and another one said, "Yeah, I don't like that either. Don't know if I like him." They do that, talk about people in 3rd person right in front of their faces. I said, "Don't they teach y'all, y'know, back in the academy days, how to stop the bleeding so somebody doesn't die?" I turned around so they could see me put my hands together like I learned you're supposed to, to stop bleeding, "You apply pressure, thusly." I did a couple of little pumps. The beat lackeys didn't like it at all. Again, they smelled. This time it was sarcasm.

But the sergeant was all set to just let me go until one of them found my baggie with its weird cargo over where I threw it. Then they all noticed I wasn't wearing my shoes. The sergeant saw the shoes a couple of yards away just sitting on the sidewalk and said, "You gettin' ready to take a foot bath?"

The fattest porkiest one held up the bloody baggie and shook it like a little glass bell and winked and said, "The bloody glove."

I said, "Those are socks."

The sergeant nodded at his thugs and walked off and drove away in his unmarked. They roughed me into the back of the squad car and rode me around for a while, not calling me in and saying, "Should we call him in?" and looking back at me and, "We could figure something else out, we could get him to talk to us friendly, get co-operative, if we get a chance to know him first," and "I don't know. Don't know if he'll make it. He might try to run." And laughing.

But after a while they chickened out of their plan to beat me up and just took me in. That's when they really found out how much they didn't like me. They had me on their trouble-maker list. I heard the complacent ugly beep coming out of their bloodless dickless geek's-best-friend. No ghost in that machine. They found out because I got cocky and gave them my real name after the front desk guy knew who the real 'Rodolphe

Desdunes' was and knew I wasn't him. Guess he didn't believe in cross-racial reincarnation.

They put me in my own private lock-up. Real modern. Recessed lights. Luxurious. They left me in there awhile but never booked me. Maybe they think crazy people are like drunks, that it'll wear off. But a man with a plan doesn't let his plan wear off.

Then I got a visitor. Not my headless info-guy. He's made himself scarce lately, ever since this dead woman's been moping around. I think one of them's taking a hankering after me. Yeah, a female, been dogging me, but I don't have time for that. Or the energy. She's too old—dead too long—for me to be interested in socially. It's kind of sick to get involved with something that's been dead that long socially. So I just ignore her, all she does is dish out the same old sad dead-people tales (they do tell 'em, man, do they). Soul resin's a different story, though, it's not even socially capable anyway. See, it's not human anymore, that's why it's OK to put it to work, a regular ghost is still human, but the resin's not sentient, it's just a memory that doesn't know how it got there.

But the resin's black and so was my living visitor, the esteemed T. Harry Williams Chair of Louisiana History, Professor Rafe Vidrine.

Jessamine Marie DuClous Bascomb

I found myself with Clara Reina at a *Bamboula*
on the Lake Ponchartrain shore. I had wrongly supposed that such practices had waned since the war
and emancipation. My first thought upon seeing the
naked Negroes writhing in obeisance to Damballa, their
snake god, was that, indeed, their hearts and minds
were not yet emancipated from the thrall of their dark
origins on the coasts of Guinea and Angola. I implored
Clara Reina to tell me why she would bring me to
such a place, to witness such an undignified display,
but she asked that I abide it and wait, that soon the
spell would begin to work its magic upon me, as it
had on her before, that I would taste fruits of untold
tartness, and that I would shortly thank her for the
excursion. So I did as she instructed and situated myself as comfortably as possible on a fallen cypress trunk,
imbibing a thick milky liquid from a gourd that was
being sent round. And, indeed, soon enough the din
of the drums began to assume an orderliness that I
previously had not perceived. Though the instruments
of their music were barbaric, indeed, fashioned crudely
out of bones and ill-tanned animal hides, broken jugs

and other manner of detritus. It was then I noticed that I was not the only white lady present, there were others, and presently one and then another rose and joined the thronging harangue of the dancers.

they have these torches it's like a weird rave and they're doing this insane drum jam, one of the slammingest grooves I ever heard? But since I can't remember any other music I've heard right now, I guess it doesn't mean much they're dancing around like Indians, like in a Kat'sina dance, but they're not, and not as much clothes, they're mostly black but there are some white people too, like the lady that's been around me a lot lately, she's sitting down and you can tell she wishes she had something to lean back against and she's fanning herself with a real old-time looking fan and she looks nervous, she also looks younger than she usually does, she's with this other lady who's creole-looking but that one's standing and kind of grooving a little bit, I bet the white lady that I guess is my friend doesn't feel right 'cause she's one of the only white people there. There are other ones but they all seem to be acting like they don't notice each other, like that time we went in that porn shop and all the guys in there from all walks of life pretend like they're the only ones in there and don't say anything to each other or act like they notice each other's there, even me. Except it's getting pretty out of control, people are getting naked and laying down in the mud 'cause it's like this field by this lake and the moon is shining on it and the temperature's really neat, sort of right there between cool and warm but then there's no temperature at all and it's like I'm just looking at it and for you the temperature's central air in your room with no windows and the fluorescent office light and the table you're in the cophouse, what did you do?

"If you came here to get my paper, I don't have it with me."

"Actually, I'm here to ask you what your paper's about."

"It's about Lucius Holt, but he's not really its most important point, it's more about, y'know, what he became."

"What does a child murdered at seventeen have a chance to become?"

"Something dead."

"Soul resin?"

The air grew warmer as the evening progressed; I surmised this was because of the heat generated by the circling, thrashing bodies of both races. Some seemed to find the climate altogether too warm for the niceties of proper dress. I suppose since the standards of public deportment were clearly being deemed suspended for the occasion, one after another of the gentlemen and ladies shed frock and shirt, then skirts and trousers, to more closely resemble, in garb if not in hue, the African cotillion which hosted them. As Clara Reina had predicted, I, too, began to feel myself being swept away by the rapture of the moment.

Indeed, I wish I were there, for this square unadorned bright room affords me no such entertainment, duty-bound though I feel to pay it its due attention. But Professor, waste not tongue nor time in the company of this derelict; simply instruct the police to detain him indefinitely. He is clearly a vagrant, a tramp. Do men not have laws anymore? And have you not means at your disposal? Social contacts?

"How'd you find out about all that evil stuff? And here I thought I was crazy."

"I've been contacted by someone from the past."

"How past?"

"A century."

"You mean a dead guy? Help! Officer! You got me in here with a psycho!"

"No, a dead woman, who knows somebody you do, or *did* know."

"Excuse me, Professor Vidrine, but fuck you. I mean it. You have no right to fuck with me that way."

my friend who's actually pretty nice to me is getting into it now, she's up there shaking it but she's kinda stiff, looks like daddy never taught her how to wiggle, but she's into it, though, she's starting to get naked like the rest of them she's getting topless and you know what, she's got a nice rack, you'd love 'em, she's all sweaty and she's rubbing herself all over and lifting her hands in the air and basically getting nasty and her hair's coming down and she looks all wavery from the firelight and the sweat and the hotness. Isn't that Vidrine you're with? I wish I could do stuff like that again, just have a conference with a prof. and pick their brains. Remember LaVonne? She was cool but whatever happened to me is her fault 'cause she's the one that told me to go out to the rez. in the first place but I wish I was sitting talking to her it would be so much mellower than anything I've done in a hundred years that's how long it feels like since I've done anything normal like just a conversation at a table with somebody that doesn't immediately morph into some other shit or just what I want to do more than anything now, just sit and burn a blunt with you in front of the tube with 'Shoba laying all over us on the couch

"Come clean with me, Mills. A woman named Jessamine Bascomb has been attempting to contact you. Have you registered her?"

"The name sounds familiar."

"She was the daughter of General Nash Newton Bascomb."

"The White League guy?"

"Yes. That may be where you remember the name from, but that's not why she's significant. Not in our time, anyway. Have you seen her?"

"What does she look like?"

"She seems to have a classical…sculpted but not bony face, very pale but with dark hair and eyebrows and rich lashes. And unusually bright, and large, gray eyes. Black hair. Seems curly but it's usually pulled back."

"There are so many of them. I really had to try to start shutting them all out awhile back just to keep from going crazy."

"Is it possible not to?"

"I don't know."

"When did you first start seeing them?"

"It was hearing them first. I think everybody does, but they just think it's their own thoughts."

"How did you find out about soul resin?"

"That was hearing, too. It really sticks out after you get used to the way everything sounds over there. It's a real commotion, right? I mean all the sounds from over there all together? Like out in the woods by some swamp right when the sun's coming down? And somebody tells you which sound the bullfrog is, and then you hear it and realize you've always heard it? Isn't that the way it is?"

"It's different for me. I haven't heard all that. I've just been told about it."

"About the soul resin, too."

"Yes. They don't don't want you tampering with it."

"Who's they?"

"Well, she doesn't, anyway."

"Who's she?"

"Jessamine Bascomb. And April Brunnen."

"There you go again. I'm not the freshman here, Socrates. Or Freud or whoever you're trying to be. You fail the quiz, sorry."

"She smells like vomit."

"The barfing lady? You mean her?"

My poor sylphide, once so balmy sweet like Autumn piney woods, came to herself with a memory of horror, for she was most ill handled, and could I shed tears I would certainly weep for her. She is called April, a name which commemorates her unspoilt former nature so much more than the bilious wretchedness she must now forever entertain. Yes, there will be times she will pass in blissful forgetfulness of the bad, she will enjoy islands of serenity as all of us in this sphere do, but they, too, will pass, to be followed by excruciating moments of her worst memory, her last, vividly relived.

now she's with this guy, first they were kind of dancing, but not really, really they were just rubbing on each other and she suddenly, like she just made up her mind, started rubbing at his dick and he started sucking on her titties like he was going crazy, really wild like, like nobody ever let him do it before and he was just losing it and he's a black guy and he's got these wide lips and a pretty big mouth 'cause he's trying to get as much tit in his mouth as possible, like trying to swallow them, with so much force she almost falls over but instead she backs up and backs up 'til she's against this tree and the guy's pressing her up against it pretty hard a tit in each hand and he's got big hands and he's squeezing them so hard they look like big eyes popping out and he's going back and forth between them with his mouth like he doesn't know which one he likes better and the look on her face is like O my God I can't believe this is happening! but in a good way a darkside hot way

I remember private youthful moments when the sight of a steed's uncovered masculinity filled me with awe and apprehension, as I wondered in girlish reveries whether the male of the human species were similarly endowed. In time I learned, but my curiosity simply shifted its focus. For then I wondered about what hungered between the legs of the unmixed Negro, certain that what lay there would more closely resemble what I had seen on horses, bulls. Many a boy in my youth had I commanded to disrobe, so that I might see, but none grown had I so instructed. But I must say my interest was that of a spectator, I simply wanted to know, to see. Not to fornicate.

she's pushing the guy off her now, he stands and looks at her for a second then he bows his head and kicks his feet at each other a couple of times then goes for her again but she pushed him off her again, she says wait I want to see you. He's not wearing a shirt but he's got pants on and he's got muddy boots on like hers, hers are muddy too and they've got little heels on them that are cool but they must be hard to walk on with the wet ground. She's holding her hand up in front of him like we used to do to tell 'Shoba to stay. Remember K-9 U? You said 'Shoba was getting his money's worth better than us at L.S.U.? And I said, you're going for free, what's your problem? And you said, yeah, they got affirmative action for white trash now but it didn't matter they just wanted better educated mercenaries and hacks but the thing to do was give 'em back something they didn't bargain on to shake 'em up or show 'em or something? Is that what you're doing now? But why? What's happened? Things are totally out of control and I don't even know what's going on anymore. But I think somebody's getting ready to get a blow-job. That lady's got the guy's pants down around his ankles she undid the buttons and lowered the pants down with her own hands but now she's stepping back and looking. Yep, pretty large thing. She's probably thinking blacksnake 'cause a lot of chicks are into that I know, she's watching it and it looks sort of a like a snake too, like a snake lifting up his head real slow and it's growing and the way it grows and is starting to point first straight ahead and now a little upward is like a snake with his one big muscle flexing and contracting to move itself along and he goes for her again but again she pushes him away and he's getting mad and too hot and he's gonna make her pay for being a bitchtease so he comes at her and she says I told you to stay away from me and she's wacking him with a stick or a cane or something from somewhere and he leaves her alone and she takes a shawl from around her waist and ties it around her chest she looks like a Mardi Gras gypsy now.

Mills Loomis Mills

Vidrine turned out to be pretty cool. Maybe he figured he could learn something off of me. I thought he bailed me out, but then I remembered there was never a charge, so I guess there was never bail. Guess he just talked them into letting me go. He asked if I'd had a good meal lately and I said, "Do I look like a bum to you?" But then I thought about it and said, "Well, I guess I do probably look like a bum to you. But you must always remember to factor in class and ethnicity when evaluating a source." I was surprised when he laughed at that.

We went to a place across the street from the lock-up, and I wanted to not eat to prove a point 'cause cops were in there, but I gave in. I *was* hungry. He said he was super hungry, too, and he said he thought it was from being in contact with the dead. I said damn straight and started to believe his story. Except the April part. I said, "Why would you expect me to believe that a girl who died in New Mexico would end up with her soul over here? It doesn't add up. Ghosts stick around where they fell."

He said, "I don't pretend to be well-versed in the theory of all this. Tell me, though. Why would a woman dead since 1876 come out of the blue with April's name?"

"I don't think she did, I think you did. To trip me up and keep me in the ranks of the losers who get done by history instead of doing it."

"Why would I want to do that?"

"'Cause you're like other historians, after writing it and thinking about it forever, you realize you haven't made it, and you don't want anyone else to 'cause you're jealous."

"It's my view that writing and thinking about history *is* making it."

He's got a lot of views like that, ones that make him look or feel like a bigger player than he is, I figure all professors do. Then he said, "But you might consider the case of Adolph Thiers."

"Who's that?"

"The French historian who so much wanted to get involved in politics. When he finally got into a position of power his only significant act was to betray his own natural constituency by brutally suppressing the Paris Commune in 1871. Now he's one of the most reviled figures in the history of his country. He would have been better remembered as a historian."

"Thanks for the free lecture. I'll remember not to suppress any communes."

"But you do plan to oppress, to exploit."

I have to say it's a pretty heavy experience having a chit-chat with Rafe Vidrine. For a historian, he's a pretty famous guy. But that's not it. It's how he talks and how he looks. He looks like one of Frederick Douglass' buddies. No beard, but he's got the white hair over the brown face—pretty impressive. And he's got the old-fahioned suits with the immaculate white shirts. Class. I used to have my shit together with the fashion statement, too, but all the the dead people stuff has disconnected me from those lesser concerns. But it's made me musty, too, like a grave or maybe just like a hippie. Yeah, like a bum. I said, "Y'know, sometimes I do feel like a bum, that's why I asked you did I look like one before."

And his eyes look like there's layers of fog moving around behind the irises.

He said, "Whether or not you're a bum is something I can't tell by looking. A bum is someone who is a parasite, or who wastes talents instilled in him not by God but by parents, or any other member of society who has reached out a hand to him. A bum is someone who leaves the world more impoverished or damaged than it was when he appeared in it."

He was right! I was in total agreement. I told him. Then I said, "That's why I've got to do what I've got to do. I mean it's a great risk to me. But the children of the future deserve it."

"What about the children of the past?"

"They're dead, professor."

"But in a way they live, you know that."

"What? Soul resin? You call that living? *Au contraire, mon frere.* Any possible change could only be better."

"But it may also affect the others. Your activation of the resin could result in something like an explosion, resulting in a vortex, or vacuum, which could turn many of the others into resin."

Yeah, he got pretty well informed from somewhere. But I said, "What? Who told you that? That dead lady? Why would you trust her over me?"

Then he really seemed to think about it. I saw it in his face the way somebody's face goes from that set little smile that says "I know what the deal is" to the frown of thinking about new possibilities, stuff you hadn't

185

thought of before. I was reaching him, all I needed to do was dig up the right tid-bit from the past: I told him, "I seem to remember you telling me what Mother Jones said, 'Pray for the dead and fight like hell for the living'."

He toppled. I saw it happen. Just a slight lift of the eyelids. He said, "I'll tell you what. It's a big world. A lot bigger all of a sudden when you start to see things the way you and I do. I taught you a few things, right?"

He waited for me to say something so I said the truth: "Definitely."

"Well, you can return the favor." He was nodding his head like from nerves and glanced everywhere around the room except at me, then at me, right in the eyes. "Introduce me to Lucius Holt."

But that idea really bothered me. I got a sudden acid reflux, my chest burned, I almost coughed. "I don't know if you wanna meet him."

"Why not?"

"He's not a very happy guy."

"I'd like to ascertain that for myself."

I thought about why it bothered me for a second and then I realized. I said, "I just wouldn't be comfortable, just because of the particulars of the case."

"Which particulars make you uncomfortable?"

I decided to lay it on the line for him. "It's the race thing."

"What about it? Then or now?"

"Well, it's about you, really. 'Cause you'll be freaked out and outraged by the racial injustice and you'll do what black people always do and reach out and blame the first whitey you see, and that'll be me."

He laughed and it sounded pretty real. I don't know 'cause I'd never seen him laugh before. Not before today but now he was laughing plenty. He said, "Oh yeah, you right, but see, I already been through that. I was born a long time before you, see. I've had plenty of time to work all that out."

So I thought it over for a second or two more and said sure. I'm not too cocky to turn down help I know I could use. Vidrine's got two things that could go a long way with me. One, he's got knowledge of the past, and I know it sounds ridiculous, but I never thought about the possibility of actually recognizing someone over there. A neat idea.

But April? Impossible. I don't know what Vidrine was trying to pull with that, but I think he's realized now that he doesn't have to bullshit me. He wants a slice of the fame, that's cool. I don't mind sharing.

Two, he's got cash, and that's a requirement to do anything. For example, a boat's gonna be required to get out to where Holt is. I showed Vidrine on the map roughly where he is, where he got killed, where Bayou Tchefuncte dumps into Barataria. No roads around there.

I said, "You wanna to meet him so bad? Let's go tonight!" And he was hip.

I know: you're thinking, "Who's putting up the blood?"

I don't know yet, but it makes sense that the one who's already had the biggest chance to do something with the first life the blood gave them would be the fairest one to donate, right? But there are other considerations. Like maybe Maya, track her down, even though she's got a lot of life in front of her, maybe she wouldn't really ever do anything with it. Or me. I know, I know, it should be me.

But what I worried about most was what he said could happen to the ghosts. No, it didn't seem too possible to me, that they would somehow get sucked into some kind of unstable expanding soul resin. And I knew better than Vidrine about dead people and all the crazy ideas they come up with. But, you know, industrial accidents do happen. Price of progress, maybe.

April Brunnen

Dear Mills: My new friend is actually turning out to be pretty cool. She's wild. Totally hip bi chick. But don't worry, I'm not going to do anything with her. Actually, we don't even talk much, she just kind of takes me around places. But I like things better now that I've met her. It's not as lonely.

Mills, don't take this the wrong way, but I think we might have to break up. No, it's not because of her. I just don't know if it makes sense anymore. I'm not solid on that, though, you could still talk me out of it. I still love you. But, you know what, it's not me, it's YOU! I just get the idea I'm not a big part of your life anymore. You don't really try anymore. You've changed. Or maybe I've changed, I don't know. Let's not do anything fast, let's take things slow, OK? Maybe we should just take a break or something?

Rafe Vidrine

The air on Broad Street was choked with exhaust, and my first feeling was that it would be nice to get out of the city, with its extra degrees of heat and humidity. My lungs felt tighter than usual, but I also had an uncomfortable claustrophobic sensation I didn't recall ever having before. The very newness of the feeling is what made it unsettling, some kind of essential opposite of *deja vu*. I felt like I was deep in the center of a huge crowd of people, that I couldn't see through them or over their heads. When I closed my eyes my mind flashed on images of them, not so much pressed together as overlapping. But even with my eyes open I would see the same scene for fractions of a second, as if from blinking, so many faces that it made all faces seem the same, more eyes than stars over the marshes, distinct points joining to form a general haze, an ashen crimson Milky Way.

I blamed the city. I noticed once more the great twin seals of the fasces boldly enshrined above the Broad Street entrance to the criminal courts building. I wanted out of the city, even if it meant with Mills and his morbid expedition. I wanted to see trees and water, not stone and smog and police officers and squad cars. But when I pictured the lazy stream, I saw an unaccountable gurgling that seemed intended as my own mind's warning not to go along. I ignored it.

Then I had other visions to contend with. The form of Jessamine Bascomb moving lightly in front of me, holding the hand of a younger and smaller woman whose image was a great deal fainter than Jessamine's. Then the voice again, like a queasy ball in my stomach, floating to me across the air currents, like a sound you hear from across the river and can't place, "Keep yourself, Professor. The adder is at your breast."

Mills asked me where my car was.

"I don't have a car."

"What, they don't let old people drive anymore? I thought y'all were running the country."

"It's my eyesight."

"Something's wrong with it?"

"Well, not anymore."

But it was deceiving me even then, because a girl I took to be ghost, the one I thought I saw walking with Jessamine, came forward quickly, stumbling over a buckling in the sidewalk, and hugged Mills like only a solid mass could.

When Mills introduced us she looked at me like she had assumed I was a run-of-the-mill Broad Street panhandler and now had to re-adjust her view. Her name was Maya. She said, "Does he know?"

Mills turned the question back on her, "Do *you* know?"

She said, "I guess."

Mills told her I was "probably wackier" than he was, therefore "in the know." She wasted no time in bringing up the subject of Mills' deceased girlfriend—not delicately, either, it seemed to me—and Mills was visibly affected. They embraced and shared some soft words. As

far as I could tell, she had taken on April Brunnen's erst-
while role. Then he asked her if she had a car and the
answer was yes.

All the while we'd been standing there a
blackshirted criminal sheriff had been watching us from
the height of the top step of criminal courts. He shouted
down at us, "Everything all right over there?"

Mills seemed to take offense, but it was always
hard to tell, ever, whether he was truly offended or just
having fun at having some justified right to be. He shouted
back, with a snide grin, "No, you got it wrong. If it's an
old white guy with two young blacks, *that's* when you
want to check it out, not the other way around." The
sheriff—who was black himself—didn't hear all of it,
but he heard enough to be offended in his own right
(that race had been mentioned at all, I assumed) and
Mills came near to being hauled right back in where
he had just come out of. The girl and I were able to
smooth things out.

Actually the girl did the talking because of my own
worsening condition. She bounded up the endless steps
and got the officer smiling. All the while Miss Bascomb
called to me in breathy whispers, more like palpable and
legible breath on my ear than sound. I contended with
this while Maya showed us to her car. Then Miss Bascomb
must have flitted off—disappeared. From this point until
after the cataclysm I heard not a peep out of her.

Mills climbed somberly into the back seat of the
little Isuzu, telling us to leave him alone. He sat in there
for an hour and wept.

Jessamine Marie DuClous Bascomb

The rain comes from all quarters of the darkest and brightest skies, and tears wet the eyes of brutes. But his tears were born of fear, not love. He worried for himself, and after a passage of long years, he came to me, there stood before me, insisting that I excuse my girl that he might speak privately. I said, "If it concerns your calling among men, it concerns the girl. Or do you still deny the bond which so plainly ties yours and her fate indissolubly together?" For he wore airs which sought to separate him from his humbler black brethren, graced as he was by ancestors as snowy as the Alpen slopes whence they hailed. He gestured at a chair and seated himself after I nodded assent. He then waited for me to offer some refreshment, but, he could not know, I had long since grown weary of observing such courtesies. I had long since wanted nothing more than to move away, to some place where one could state bluntly what one wished and be told, without negotiation, whether such was possible. As I never learned of the existence of such a place, I remained in New Orleans. At least I could indulge my craving for rudeness with the once

rising, now bumbling Clouet. I said, "What do you
want from me?"

He sighed feebly as if in recognition of insult,
though he knew he must endure it with grace. He
then amused me with a request for an audience with
my father. This caused me to smile more broadly than
either I or, I assumed, my guest had in some time. "My
father is not accustomed to entertaining gentlemen of
your persuasions," then I thought to add an inescap-
able detail—"or hue." I knew from the cast of his face
that the *bête politique* was at work on him, so I extended my remarks: "Why did I not have the good
fortune to know one of the great Creoles of your race?
Really, not even Pinchback would be disloyal enough
to seek out an association with the beast of Harmony
Street."

At this his color became actually darker, but before he got far in a stormy display of feigned outrage,
he thought better of insulting me with his political
charades. He seated himself once more and requested
my permission to smoke. Once granted, he reflected
for a few moments and then began his ascent to the
lofty rostrum of speechifying. "Your father is a man of
unswerving will. The strength of his convictions is so
great that it finds itself uncomfortable in what he, himself, has called the 'grayness' of our republican institutions. Indeed, for a man of Bascomb's single-
mindedness, the democratic call to mediation and compromise must appear plainly unheroic, uninteresting.
He sought first in armed rebellion to preserve his antiquated right to absolute power, though it meant the
destruction of the only free nation on earth. After having been fairly whipped on the battlefield, he now
seeks the self-same goals he has ever sought through
means more treacherous even than war. He has taken
to secret plotting, subterfuge, even to hiring assassins

to complete the work he is too cowardly to undertake himself—"

Undoubtedly "Narcisse" would have ranted on forever thus, but I interrupted him with a protest— "Why do you take me for one of the ignorant Negroes you seek to inflame with such talk? The effect is surely lost upon me, for I do not care how my father chooses to pass his time, be it at cards or politics, and I fail to grasp in what way you, yourself, are exempt from the charges you bring against Bascomb."

"I have ever stood for Progress."

"Ah, yes, the hundred-footed chimera round every bloodletting's bend. My father claims to know him, too."

"The Constitution of the United States is no chimera."

"No? And did you sing the Battle Hymn of the Republic so loudly when you, like Nash Bascomb, wore the gray? At least my father never enslaved his own race."

"Your father, like all of his class, enslaves his own race every day."

More of his Jacobinism. He then exclaimed, "You persist in thinking of me as a Negro," and his great annoyance shone through. "Your provincialism becomes you not."

"Pray, monsieur, what does become me?"

He sighed and brought his hand to his chin, in a show of contemplation, then grinned lecherously.

"Perhaps you feel it becomes me to display in my parlor a grinning half-breed in overzealous finery."

"If it pleasures mam'sell to think so."

"You disgust me."

I had become quite piqued and found myself in a confused state of mind. All manner of contumely raced about my head and begged the privilege of utterance. I wanted him either to quit my presence and languish, indeed, perish, out of my sight, or that he should avenge

his outraged honor upon my body. He sought to match
his eyes with mine and spoke my name. The sound of it
and the sight of the rich and delicate woman's mouth
speaking awakened desires in me I had long thought deceased. Shakespeare had it that fortune was a strumpet. Desire is the strumpet.

I said, all too aware of the barely restrained tremolo
of my voice, "It must have caused you no end of satisfaction to enjoy your *cinq à sept* refreshment with the
daughter of your enemy."

"I have not forgotten, Jessamine," he replied in a
softer tone, "but it injures me to hear you speak so
disdainfully of the most sacred fulfillment I have ever
felt. You mention your father. I wish we both could
forget him. You mention your father."

"Narcisse" Clouet faltering in his declamations?
And there it was, there was the tear in his eye, and
making its solitary trek down his golden, paraffin cheek.
My newly rediscovered affections were checked, however, when he revealed the cause of his tears. "Your
father is bent on my murder, he plots it even as we
speak."

I have never enjoyed the sensation of pity, so I
sought to spurn it from me, though it tugged with great
insistence. I rose and poured for myself a claret, though I
failed to invite my supplicant to join me. I stood and
held my gaze upon him, downward, and his eyes sought
mine and lingered there. What had been tears hardened
into thick glass, the eyes I remembered, those which appraised and acquired and sold off again, though they knew
they could be plucked out at the most libertine whim of
fortune. I was caught up in an inner swoon, a humid
breeze, but I maintained my outward composure. He
would not have a trembling girl this time.

I said, "As to your future, it is quite beyond my
purview to make you guarantees." And then my tongue

of its own volition resolved what my heart and mind could not. "As to our past, why banish to the past what may be re-enacted for the present?"

He fell on bended knee before me and pressed my hand against his cheek. I know that I never surrendered my composure, which undoubtedly irked him, though surely not enough utterly to spoil the memory of the experience. I suppose Narcisse cherishes what he has, what he was left with, as all of us do. There are no enemies in our mild hell, only the fear of losing those final threads of recollection. I feel already the black swoon commandeering all the footpaths of my memory, like spreading spilt ink, it hems me in.

Rafe Vidrine, from Beyond Yellow and Black: Franco-African Political Culture in New Orleans

In November 1864, when the Quadroon Bill proposed to count all Lousianians with a quarter or less black blood as white, Clouet opposed it—even though he might easily have qualified. He took this stand in concert with the other leading creole radicals, with whom he had not yet broken. At the convention which assembled on January 9, 1865, Clouet is said to have spoken in glowing terms of the diversity of cultural background, occupation, educational attainment, and means evidenced at Liberty Hall. He was still closely associated with Louis Roudanez' radical *New Orleans Tribune*, which wrote of the convention:

> There were seated side by side the rich and the poor, the literate and educated and the country laborer, hardly released from bondage, distinguished only by the natural gifts of the mind. There the rich landowner, the opulent tradesman, seconded motions offered by humble mechanics and freedmen. Ministers of Gospel, officers and soldiers of the U.S. army, men who handle the sword or the pen, merchants and clerks,—all the classes of society were represented

and united in a common thought: the actual libera-
tion from social and political bondage.

(*Tribune* January 15, 1865)

The lack of attention to color in the above statement, with emphasis instead frankly on class, is typical
of the creole champions of color-blind and egalitarian
citizenship. However, after the 1866 riot, which Clouet
only narrowly escaped with his life, he began to move
toward racial conservatism. This was exceedingly pre-
mature, since radical congressional Reconstruction had
not yet even begun. The next half-decade or so would be
the radicals' brief hour. Perhaps Clouet saw in 1866 a
vignette of the more widespread carnage of the 1870s and
onward.

Mills Loomis Mills

So Maya was loitering around on Broad looking for trouble. Looking for me. She said, "Omigod, they let you out!"

I said, "Hey, try to sound more upbeat."

"I am, I thought they were going to bust you for that guy."

"Thank this guy," I said, and introduced her to the inestimable Vidrine. She looked totally baffled that I would ever hang out with either a black guy or an old guy. I wish my generation wasn't so superficial and stupid and cliquish. I'm not bashing Maya, though. I guess I have to say she's pretty awesome. My only regret here on the edge of the chasm is that I didn't make time to fuck her first. But then again that might've been too creepy because she said, straight-up, right there on the sidewalk, "Is April the name of somebody you used to go with?" Vidrine shot me a look full of buckshot, but I pretended it all missed me. I said, "Well, it sounds like y'all are more in touch with them than I am, so why don't y'all just go do it."

I was just bullshitting, but Maya said, "April says maybe you shouldn't do it."

"Do what?"

"Something that this friend of hers says could make things really bad for all of them."

"All of who?"

"The other ones, y'know." She waved her hands around with her head bowed and glaring at me like we were trying to keep something from the kids.

The problem was, I couldn't tell whether Maya was really down with the soul scene or just generally tripped out. I said, "What does this April look like?" And she did a harumph like I just insulted her intelligence.

But then she got mellow and said, "Mills? You don't know?" And she gave me a big hug right there on the street. Vidrine turned away like polite repressed bourgeois types do when people get lubby-dubby. I was thinking up a good wisecrack about how Maya was tripped out of her mind and wasting my time, but then she said, "No wonder you don't want to see her." And I couldn't help it, I got fucked with by another emotion wave, memory, that was the culprit. April again, this time just moving a plant from one windowsill to another one and humming and smiling at me a regular everyday throwaway domestic smile. I said, "Is that what she thinks? I don't wanna see her?"

"Sometimes." She was still hugging me and I went along with it. I had my face pressed into her shoulder so Vidrine couldn't see my face all twitchy and scrunched up like a baby. "She doesn't really know what's going on, though. I don't think she totally knows what's up. She's confused."

Then this cop hollered some bullshit at us, and I had to tell him what time it was. He said he'd lock me up and I said good idea and I meant it—because I started to believe that April really was out there, and I figured then I should try to see her before making the trip. Find out what I might be getting myself into. But it didn't happen 'cause Vidrine and Maya talked him out of it. What was that Thoreau said about how friends should mind their own business and go ahead and let the law fuck with you?

We made Maya's car and I asked her and Vidrine to let me just sit in there alone a minute. I was in there more like thirty minutes. I saw April but I didn't talk to her. I couldn't. She kept saying, "Can't you hear me?" and talking crazy like she didn't know she was dead. Horrible. And she's all…she looks bad. But I guess she can't feel it now, or anything. But lots of times she suddenly screams and thrashes around and kicks. She's probably trying to get out of the woman she's sort of lodged in. I think it's one I've seen before. I remember wondering why she picked such an elaborate outfit to die in.

Not like April. April's naked. A lot of them are. Those are the ones you most don't want to look at. Something about being dead and being naked makes me sick, like great-looking food that you're getting ready to eat and you find out when you look close there's maggots swimming around in it. And she had blood on her and she looked like she'd been dragged around in mud, or even maybe buried. But she just kept talking at me. Both of them, her and the other lady. April was mad at me, like I'd cheated on her or something and she was talking to me about it like she was dressed and sitting in some nice restaurant dragging on an argument cigarette. I wanted one too. But I had to talk. I couldn't just ignore her.

I asked her, "So why did you come back to New Orleans then?"

"You cruel fucking bastard," she spat, "why didn't you get off your ass and make some money and come out to see me in New Mexico? We could have been together. Everything could've been different. I'm back here 'cause I wanted to see you, OK? I'm a nerd, OK?"

She got distracted and started digging her fingers into a gross gash in her soft downy abdomen, where there wasn't much dirt. Yeah, put there by a knife, sword, meat cleaver, chainsaw, whatever. But to her it was like picking at a fingernail.

I said, "Doesn't that hurt?"

"No, it's cool, I can't feel it. I just want to check it out. You've seen me do worse."

I had? I guess she meant flicking boogars or something.

"But hey, April, **how** did you get here?"

She didn't seem to know what "how" meant. She stared.

"Plane, train, boat?"

"Well, you know, it's like I said. In my letter? Did you even read them? It's like solid over in New Mexico and here it's water. Like what's rock over there is liquid here."

"The Apache Tears?"

"Whatever." She snorted. "You don't need to label every last thing."

I'd never seen her this bitchy before, but I liked it. She used to stick up for herself about as much as a wet futon on 'ludes. And here was this take-no-shit snide-ass. I almost told her I liked how she grew up, but I thought it would depress her, 'cause she'd have to say, "Shame I'm not still alive, what a waste."

She was still trying to figure out how she got here. "You just slide sort of down the rock and then it turns crystal and then this sticky stuff like bubblegum, then just regular water. Mud first, no, clay first, then mud, then water. That's what it feels like all the time now. Just water. Not too clear water. Hard to breathe. It's all light-headed like there's not enough oxygen and you never know if you're suffocating or not. New Mexico's rock and air and here is mud and water. This is a shitty place to be."

"April—"

"But I came here to see you. I knew you were here, and you know what? You were thinking of me when I died. I did, I died." She tugged at a curl of hair and wrapped it around her finger like she used to do when she was thinking melancholy stuff. And she almost faded away. But I whined her name and she perked up again. "And I busted half an ass to get here and now…well, I guess it's cool to see you."

And the other lady just kept yapping at me about leave the soul resin alone, I could hurt people.

Hurt people? Dead people? They've already been hurt.

April Brunnen

Jessamine says it'll be bad, but I don't see how. She told me how to feel it and I can now. It's like a pull down in the stomach. The weird thing is, after I thought about it, it hit me that it's the only thing I feel, I mean all the time, when I'm not dreaming. It's all like a dream, but sometimes it's more dreamy than the rest of the time. It's more dreamy feeling when I'm hanging back with you or other people from before. Things are different now and I know they'll always be this way, the way they are now. Jessamine says it could be worse but I think she's fulla shit. "It could be worse" is one of the dumbest things anybody can say. I bet you agree with that. You know how when you're sleeping in and you're sort of half-awake and you really want to get up but these half-dreams keep pulling you back into a half-sleep where you can't get up and move around really, like you want to? That's what it's like. I don't like it. I like days I never thought I liked before. I'm sorry about Linguistics. It was your idea to take it pass/fail and just show up for the mid-term and the final. I knew he would give me a break if I went in there without you because I guess that's how male profs are. But if I went in there with you and we both said we missed the mid-term then he would know we were in it together and maybe missed it on purpose 'cause how's he supposed to know that two people are such major slackers that they'd both space the date? And also he'd know we were together and he wouldn't be able to have his little disgusting fantasies about me. I'm sorry. It's been nice seeing you, really great. But I don't see how things could work out anymore. We've sort of grown apart, that's all. I need different things now and probably so do you.

Charles Cannon, from Soul Resonance: A History of the Great Rift and its Consequences for the Living and the Dead

Rafe Vidrine never had a middle name. He was an orphan, left in a fruit crate under an abandoned church in Petit Bois, Louisiana, in 1944. He was discovered by some white children who had converted the former black church into what they called a "hideout." James Odum remembered the incident eighty years later. "It used to be we was playing G.I.s, y'know, what with the war. But then we got a little older and bored with the other thing, like happens with boys. So then we made like we was bankrobbers and it was our hideout from the G Men."[2] Their play consisted of shoplifting at a local store and then hoarding the loot—candy, matches, shoelaces—in the dilapidated church. One morning they discovered that their retreat had been used by others during the night: there were potted meat tins and empty beer bottles. Some of the hoarded candy had been consumed. This mystery sent Odum's playmate to get a BB gun while Odum climbed up onto a rotting rafter to keep a lookout through the little window facing to the

---

[2]This may seem like a retroactive progression, but that's what my aged witness reported.

front. What he chanced to see were two white men he didn't recognize, standing behind adjacent trees in a tangled bottom thicket on the far side of the road, both staring intently at the church. The boy concluded that his gang's hideout had been found out. He feared that if he stayed where he was and if those men chose to return, he'd easily be discovered and cornered inside the building. So he sneaked down and dropped through one of the great holes in the floor onto the earth below—the structure was raised three feet off the ground on brick pilasters. This is when he saw the infant, sleeping in a fruit crate propped against the back of the brick steps leading to the sanctuary.

It was a black child, a boy. The boys took him home, and he was then conveyed to the nearest black church, which housed the congregation once worshipping at the abandoned building, *Ebenezer A.M.E.*

Notices were placed in the local paper as well as in the New Orleans papers, but the only fruit they yielded was an anonymous scrawled memo: *"His name is **Rafe**."*

He was adopted by a middle-aged childless couple who attended *Ebenezer*, William and Nell Vidrine.

Although he was not informed of his adoption until after his adoptive parents' deaths, Vidrine speaks of always having a sense that some segment of his life had already taken place before he ever knew the Vidrines.[3] He never felt what he describes as "normal familial intimacy," and he characterized his parents' affections as "bureaucratic." However, he has also admitted that he never remembered much at all from the first ten years of his life—not before the Rift, that is, which brought back his early memory.

---

[3]This although he was less than a year old when he was discovered under the old church.

The best thing the Vidrines did for him (besides feeding, clothing and housing him) was to move to New Orleans when Rafe was ten. This move was fortuitous for Vidrine for two reasons: first, the education he was able to get in the city made the fundamental difference in what would turn out to be a scholarly life. But equally or perhaps more important was his exposure in New Orleans to a black political culture which would provide the rhetorical fuel to energize and inspire the young Vidrine to what he has called "the life of the political mind." No, Vidrine never ran for or held public office. Vidrine has always believed that acts of the intellect are just as much "actions" as physical, political, or more directly social "action." To the criticism of his peers that he was not active enough in the Civil Rights Movement, he responded that his efforts to rewrite official U.S. history (to correct it, that is) were equally as "activist" as a protest march or boycott.

Jessamine Marie DuClous Bascomb

The last time I saw my father he wore a mask. It was a great head of a gorilla or chimpanzee, or some other like ape, but the color was an unlikely bright yellow. He sat upon an oversized chair which made his form seem as that of a child's. In his hand, or "paw," I should say, was a great lollipop in the likeness of a banjo. His collar and cuffs were grossly oversized, as was a quite ridiculous hat which wobbled precariously with every lurch of the horses: for it was carnival, and he sat upon a float and paraded in this manner through the streets. The brightly festooned wagon which bore him also featured another, lower tier which carried other monkey-men—these black or brown, rather than yellow, and clothed in costume bearing a striking resemblance to those worn by Clouet's militia. Painted in gauche, childlike alphabet along the section of float nearest the wheels were the words, "NOO LOO-SANA UMM-BUS," and a blue star was depicted there, also, like the stars on those omnibus lines before the war offering passage to quadroons, etc., as well as white. I knew it was Bascomb, because the Krewe, after all, was Comus, and the mock French confabulation of

ugly guttural noises emanating from beneath the el-
ephantine ape head sounded too much familiar with
my father's drunken mockery of my mother and all
her people. The draped banner above him read "Tableau IX—Political Evolution."

Yes, and there competing with the parade in a contest to banish the night's darkness in a revel of lights was
the rotunda of the St. Charles Hotel. Here my father
also kept rooms, and lo, there he waved his candied scep-
ter at many a knowing wink upon the balconies. I dared
not follow further, no matter how great my preposter-
ous curiosity regarding my father's role in the play, for
the parade's continuing route past the gambling parlors,
saloons, shooting galleries, and theatres was no place for
a prudent woman to be on a night such as this, with the
men of the world carousing happily and without a care,
their identities safely concealed.

'73? Surely not, for by then had I not certainly made
Clara Reina my steadfast companion? Did we not go
about carnival always together? We certainly never
ventured beyond Canal Street. Of all the close-quartered
faces of my memory, hers is most reluctant to pay me a
visit. Why, I do not know. Probably I've forgotten an
incident of the gravest importance. I remember some,
though. She sang. She sang mad Lucia at the opera, with
a traveling company who refused to bar her from their
stage as the Uptowners did. I feared her, and could not
speak to her after the performance. Her face all a question, the color rising in her cheeks, so like her brother's,
and the same rash leap to rage as well, she thundered,
"Did you not enjoy my singing?" I remember her *atelier*,
always with flowers, white for Sundays, red for Fridays.
She joked that she had not yet found black blooms, alas
not even gold. I said I could locate for her a yellow. Was
she amused? I remember her Schubert, and mine, for I
had not forgotten my piano lessons, though my hands

trembled at the keys. We had a fondness for swings draped from the boughs of trees. We passed many hours with our skirts tucked and tied, our shoes flung off, the tips of our toes thrusting at the heavens, be they black, pink, azure.

I remember also starting up from an evening *sieste* in my reading chair to the sound of her urgent heels upon the stair, to a whiff of her summer silks through the door. There she stood before me, her face flushed, droplets of sweat upon her upper lip which appeared master-sculpted as ever. And her multitude of showering ringlets of hair, they were like yours, dear sylph, only black rather than red.

"Spring Queen!" I cried, for this was my affectionate name for her. "Is it to me that you hurry so?"

She said it was, but fell suddenly to weeping. "Jessamine," she spoke in broken whispers, "this world was not made for us." I nodded assent without hesitation. But then added, "Whatever do you mean?" for though I agreed in general, indeed, *in toto*, I longed to know which particular incompatibility between the world and ourselves she alluded to.

"Your father and my brother, even now they fire upon each other, at Liberty Place."

I made to speak, to assert my view that the antics of our masculine relatives need not necessarily concern us so, but she turned her black eyes on me with such bitter recrimination that I remained silent.

We passed the remainder of the evening mourning together, silently, our sad, separate futures.

Mills Loomis Mills

I laid out the plan. First stop: KB booze mart for my fortification. Two: Security Sporting Goods to buy a nasty looking "fishing" knife and some line (they had a nice one with a bone handle). Three: Earl's Bar to rent a boat and a trailer.

Vidrine put up the capital for all this. He looked like a guy in an AMEX commercial. Maya's Hyundai had lots of trouble pulling the boat (a tiny skiff with the smallest outboard they had), but around dusk St. Claude turned into St. Bernard, and then we were turning off down a shell road and riding it till it was a soggy promontory sinking into a windy desolation of brown shallow water. Restless bored ripples all over it. The main birds weren't egrets or herons or fantastic water eagles—they were buzzards, come to eat these skinned nutria carcasses floating around in the thin brown soup like biology class specimens in formaldehyde. At least it gave me the opportunity to prove decisively a controversial question: no, ratty animals like that don't have souls. Well, not ones that last anyway. Maya was deep-six bummed by the poor animals, though. She said it made her sick, made her want to throw up. "Just get me outta here," she said, "and I'm up for whatever."

I said, "Can't you smell it? Feel it?"

"I'm worried that whatever I smell is those nutrias."

"No," I tried to do a patronizing smile, but she didn't seem to get it. A strange rustle in the wind kicked up and wiped over us and I asked her. "How do you feel?"

"I just feel scared."

"That's it," I said. "How do you feel, professor?"

He didn't look too chipper. He just nodded. He didn't say anything else until I had pretty single-handedly dragged the boat off the trailer and then I realized the water was too shallow there—and probably a lot of places—for the outboard to work. Shoulda gotten an air-boat. Duh. Then Vidrine talked. Wanted to know where we were going and what I intended to do. I said, "You wanted to meet Lucius Holt, didn't you?"

He didn't exactly nod, but he didn't shake his head either.

"Soon enough he'll be all over the place. I've got a line on him right now."

"A line?"

"Hm-mm. I can feel where he's at."

Maya was in a realistic mood. She said, "How are we going to get there?" She'd figured out too that the outboard would just dig a big hole in the silt and then clog up and choke and die. The Professor was standing around looking like it was his first day on planet earth, more spaced out than the guy who invented flubber. All he had to say was, "Really quiet out here."

Rafe Vidrine

For the first time in days, Jessamine Bascomb was nowhere to be seen. I didn't feel crowded anymore, but I was still uncomfortable. The air was saturated with a tense, forced peace. I found I was sweating, anxious. But I also began to realize why I was there, why I had come along, why I was willing to participate, full of zombie-like submission, although I was sure I should be against the whole enterprise. I began to feel that my role here was scripted, that whatever the outcome, I had to get through it because not to participate would be the more irresponsible choice. But I also began to feel that what was going to happen would be connected to my personal life, to my personal past, in fact. The name of Lucius Holt began to have an utterly different kind of resonance than it had ever had before. Did I know him? This place, this windswept dead-end in this marsh, this water, I remembered it. Of course, one weak patch of delta mud looks pretty much like the next one, and the one a hundred miles away. But lights started going on in places in my mind that had slept for fifty years—memories.

My uncle used to take me fishing. Often. We went for crawfish. I had forgotten. It could have been here.

Then we stopped coming out. It was because of me. Because I would panic for no reason. Beg for him to take me home. I felt a slithering in the sandy shallows, my mind possessed by visions of bloody torture, unheeded cries for mercy, laughter. At first my uncle tried laughter, too, probably hoping that it would show me how baseless my fear was. I could see him, in memory, standing in the skiff, his arms outstretched, turning his head successively in all directions: "Rafe? Ain't nothing out here." Until he saw it just made me panic more wildly. Until I would leap from the boat and stumble awkwardly though water and grasses in no sensible direction—like an injured dog who runs from the pain he feels. He would catch me and drag me back—"Now you go tearing up on a gator nest, you will get yourself killed"—how often?

Mills shook me by the shoulder. "It must be the books have got to you this time, 'cause the real goners would be crazy to be anywhere near here."

"Where have they gone?"

Maya said, "They can't be around here because of the soul resin, right? 'Cause it could make things worse for them?"

"Maya can feel it," he said, "right?" She nodded. She looked apprehensive—as I'm sure I did.

I said, "Is it in the stomach?"

Maya nodded as Mills looked out over the quietly rippling water.

"A dull ache?"

Mills said that was it, ran his finger through the water and tasted it.

"Is it Lucius Holt?"

He didn't answer. When Maya asked who Holt was, Mills said, "Got your lecture notes, doc?"

Maya looked at me, but I didn't answer. Mills was cutting a thick switch out of a reed. He said, "Don't worry about it Maya. Holt doesn't matter."

222

I said, "He does matter," but couldn't say why.

Mills lay the switch on the water and watched it float out.

Maya said, "He's a guy who bled once and he's the one that's making us feel sick. But he doesn't even know it. He's just a kid. He doesn't know why he's bleeding, I mean, he thinks he doesn't deserve it. He's really pissed."

Mills sighed dramatically. "He's not anything anymore, you're just getting the leftover static. Think of it like a message from another galaxy that they sent fifty years ago but we're just getting it now."

She said, "No. He is there. Just not much of him. Just one tiny bad part of him that can't move."

Mills: "Well, sure, that could be one way of putting it, yeah."

We all got in the boat and shoved off, leaving the outboard at road's end. Mills rowed, often jerking his head fitfully in the air like a hound trying to pick up a scent. All around at eye level and above was vast mottled gray sky. All I heard at first were oars in water, our creaking boat, our own breath, and marsh grasses bending to the wind.

April Brunnen

Jessamine's turning out to be a major drag, she acts like she can control me. But it sucks 'cause I think maybe she can. I wish I could figure out a way to get away from her. I know I said I wasn't sure about you and me anymore but I didn't mean like cold turkey, I thought we could still spend time together but she won't let me and now I don't even know if you're around anymore or where you went 'cause when you drove off with that girl and Professor Vidrine she told me I couldn't go. I said hey you're not my mom, back off, and she told me some b.s. lecture that I couldn't even figure out *Do you not remember how you came to be here? To follow him would be to risk returning to the arms of your murderer, forever. Is this the honey-moon you desire?* It wasn't Mills, shut up! Why do you think you know anyway? You can't read my mind *Child we have the same mind, though I make no claim as to its legibility* It was in a whole different state, it was the Land of Enchantment, and Louisiana is the Dream State and I'm dreaming now but I don't know what state I'm in but Mills loves me, he loves me, he's the only one who's ever loved me and he'd never hurt me and

I want to be with him *He lives, April, he lives and you can never again be with him because you are dead* Fuck you, no I'm not, let me go.

Jessamine Marie DuClous Bascomb

It appeared to be a span of cooperage loosed from a cartwheel. It must have been difficult to wield, for the brigand had constantly to shift the instrument in his hand to get a trustier grip. He had beaten his victim so severely about the face with it that even a dear friend would not be able to ascertain the bloody man's identity. At least I assumed it was a man. His clothes were masculine, and they were also of fine tailoring: a gold brocade vest— from which a fine rose-gold watch was removed—and a white linen frock coat which would never be cleansed of the great splotches of gory blood about the shoulders. I could not ascertain the man's race, his hands alone would not tell it, but he seemed a bit slight of build to be my Narcisse, whom I presently worried over more than I ever thought I would. I honestly had not realized that his enemies were so many and so dedicated in their unlawful purpose. I discovered the degree to which these malefactors would throw common Christian decency to the winds when I sought once, in the sulphurous mist of that wanton morning, to intercede.

It happened when the mounted horsemen, most wearing at least one vestige of Confederate raiment, spurred their beasts onto the square, leaving behind them an assortment of the oldest and weakest, those who fell before the steeds and sought vainly to dodge the murderous hooves. The groaning remainder who lay in the wake of the "cavalry" was then set upon by common street ruffians—Irish, I assumed. I could stand idly by no longer when two lads of school age had propped up an old mammy against a horsepost and then took turns leaping up and kicking her in the face with their boots, in a gruesome game of target practice. More boys joined in the play, it being the duty of the youngest—whom I assumed to be not older than five years—to prop the old crone back upright against the post to await her next kick. When I endeavored to put a stop to their barbaric contest, I was informed that I would be next. I was told that when they "got done with all the niggers" that it would then be the turn of the "scally-wag meddlers" and the "French whores." Still, I persisted until an older boy seized me and proclaimed his intention to make me know what it meant to be French and woman. I must confess that my fear was great, yet I was more enraged than terrified. I know not whether it was quivering spine or rising bile which caused me to invoke the name of my father. It was then that I noticed a Boylan's policeman who had been leaning against the brick of Edelmann's cigar store, enjoying the parade, it seemed, until the name Bascomb woke him to his duties. He then strode briskly into the melee and struck with his baton at the man grasping me until he desisted. The policeman then took off his hat to me and begged pardon. I knew then the identity of our host, the sponsor of the day's festivities. It was a Bascomb affair, at which I was, of course, an honored guest.

After I learned this, the goings-on before me appeared in a most confusing light, because I no longer feared for my own person, yet I wondered whether my signature, too, would seal the carnage still waxing in the Mechanic's Institute square. The little man who suffered the beating of wagon-wheel iron, the row of men on their knees falling sharply forward after pistol blasts to the head. The white man—was it Durant?—who was held upright by two jeering monsters in Confederate caps (they appeared to be Mississippians), while a third opened up the belly with a dagger, unraveling guts and lifting them up with the tip of the offending blade so that the dying man could behold his own innards. It was as if this scene was simply a matter of quotidian triviality, my sense was that this was the common manner of society in this quarter and that I had simply not visited the neighborhood before—like the Confederate grays and butternuts that had not been seen for so long, they were suddenly here again: quite obviously, they had never been away. How naive was it for one such as I to think that the Martian bloodlust would be satiated with the souls of Vicksburg and Shiloh. It must come here, it must feed upon the innocents of a city desirous of peace, and even then is its appetite only whetted. What strikes down an armed soldier on the battlefield must then try its hand at an unarmed woman, must then lust to skewer babes. And when I recognized, in the pattern of terror and blood so rudely smeared before me, the name Bascomb, I searched all the more desperately for Clouet. However, he, of all people, this scrape he survived well, injured in pride only, though not in body. For this was not Liberty Place, and I still lived.

Charles Cannon, from Soul Resonance: A History of the Great Rift and its Consequences for the Living and the Dead

Maya Vracar's role in the Rift and in Mills' life remains fairly shadowy. In all years since the Rift, she has continued in her strict reclusiveness. To all appearances she rarely leaves the boundaries of her ranch in New Mexico—she has not been seen in public at all for ten years. It is probable that she first met Mills only shortly before November 23. Mills' tapes indicate the need for an assistant—they also suggest that he once planned to use the blood of an unsuspecting victim to activate the soul resin. Whatever the reasons for their association, it was fortuitous in that Vracar turned out to be a highly intuitive medium. She perceived Jessamine Bascomb only a few hours after Mills introduced her to his view of the world and to the possibility of interlocution with departed souls. She was the first living person to sight April Brunnen, at a time when her shade was barely perceptible even to the dead.

Years later, in her brief role as pitch celebrity for *Tele-Psychic Fast Forward,* she would credit her great sensitivity to the early death of her mother and her subsequent rearing by grandparents. These grandparents had enjoyed an active social life which exposed the young

Maya to elderly personalities who then died—the girl then felt and expressed a sense of continued contact with some of the deceased family friends. At a certain age her reports on the relative welfare of these dead were discouraged, so she began to neglect her unusual communicative faculty. It remained dormant until she began to experiment with psychedelic drugs as a teenager. These experiences loosened up her perceptual apparatus as well as her moral inhibitions forbidding alternative forms of perception and communication. But at the time she met Mills Loomis Mills she was apparently still unsure what was hallucination and what was true ghost.

Rafe Vidrine met Vracar for the first time on November 22, when he bailed Mills out of jail. She had been waiting in her car. His first impression of her is telling—he thought she was a ghost. Her car provided the transport to the jumping-off point at the terminus of Old Tchefuncte Road.

Rafe Vidrine

I remember Mills remarking that we were still far off, explaining that the water's currents were still being driven by wind and gravity, while close to the soul resin the water would be sucked toward the location of Lucius Holt's blood remains. Other than Mills' reports, none of us talked. What I heard then was the dipping of the oars, seagull bleating, the occasional rattling of a king-fisher, a woodpecker hammering away at a dead cypress, and the pervasive hum of marsh insects, which got louder and joined by frogs as the twilight deepened. The bayou narrowed, or maybe its banks just became better defined since trees now grew on either side. The trees added a descant of birdsongs to the low groundswell of bugs and amphibians. An alligator cow bellowed not far off. A close-by owl and a distant one traded their hooted rhythms. I was startled by a large bird who suddenly broke with the sameness of color behind it and sprung into the air. I assumed it to be a heron. The bright white of the egrets stuck out more, even to my weak vision, though they stood as stock still as the tree-stumps. The bayou widened out, and the trees closed in. We found ourselves not in any kind of stream at all anymore, but in a broad swamp. Mills continued more or less along the same trajectory, but the timber was too crowded to row, so we pulled ourselves along by grabbing onto the cypress trunks, whose crowns looked to me like shadows painted on the bland starless sky. After an hour of this Mills and Maya Vracar jumped out into the knee-high water and pushed the boat forward and over fallen trunks and underwater bushes.

I stayed in the boat, feeling like an invalid. I wanted to help but I suffered from an irrational and paralyzing fear of the water. The boat struck me as rusted and stationary, though it was neither. I was visited by a stubborn vision of a cluster of white men poking and prodding and slicing a bound black man, on a creaking boat at an unseaworthy angle, they dangled me over the water, and I felt relief every time they didn't drop me.

Maya Vracar asked Mills if he knew where he was going.

"The way that drone is building," he said, "as soon as we get into clear water we'll be able to ditch the oars and just float right in."

Maya asked, "What drone?"

"Don't you hear it? Listen under all the swamp racket."

I listened too. After a process of elimination I knew which sound he meant, the sound I couldn't account for. I thought of a way to describe it, "Like a farm sound, a cow with a bloated udder, lowing, but tape-recorded and played at a slower speed."

"Bingo, farmer Brown."

Maya admitted hearing it too. It seemed to get louder as we proceeded but was impossible to point to. It got louder but always seemed to be all around us. At first it simply stood out in bolder relief from the other, more typical, wetland sound canopy. Then it appeared to subsume parts of it, a cicada here, a bullfrog there, like a vortex, a great orchestral gong banged louder every time until even its overtones outweighed the other instruments.

Maya Vracar said, "That's trippy, but since when does it sound like blood?"

"Since it became something greater than just blood, since it made the leap from some cheap body's spilled life to a fancy car made of all the time in the world."

Mills continued manufacturing flashy explanations, most of them full of a perverse love of death, but I was too worried about myself to listen. And, yes, I was touched by the seduction, too. I felt the resin, too. It started in at the ears and quickly coursed throughout the entire body, soaking you from within. I strained my eyes to see something that might cause such a sensation. I was convinced that whatever it was had to be big—I envisioned a giant lizard, a godzilla rearing up suddenly out of the swamp with a piece of the Empire State Building in his mouth. But all I saw was a thinning of trees, a basin spreading out under an upturned bowl of gray soup, with its clouds languishing like overcooked cauliflowers. Yet our boat lurched forward with new vigor. I heard the thud of Mills pulling the oars in. The boat gained enough speed to put breezes on our faces. I smelled cigar smoke and cheap booze breath. Thought I tasted grape soda in my mouth, but they could never make me drink it, not even when I was a kid. So how do I know what it tasted like? Then I thought of Mattie LaVonne. I knew she wanted me to stay alive. What would she think? What was I doing?

Mills Loomis Mills

My ribcage is vibrating like a tuning fork. The booming throb of the soul resin is soaking me like a yawning foghorn, and me into the mouth, as small as a tanker spit into the gulf. But I know I got enough ammo—eight pints of it—to get into the stomach of the thing and explode my way out.

We were drudging through this swamp, but then the trees slacked off, it looked like river again, or lake, it was open water where you could see and feel broad ripples of unblocked current, wake, sparked by what? That's when I knew we had never lost the Tchefuncte.

Then I saw them, rickety awkward shapes about a hundred yards off. Nothing like trees. They were lower, stiller, grimmer. Jagged. They looked like a comic-book sillouhette of a shattered skyline. I knew they couldn't be anything but a bunch of old boats. When we pulled in a little closer we could hear some of them, creaking and whispering and snuggling their rusty hulls together. Comforts of the dead—at least the boats still had physical form. A cloud moved out from in front of the moon and we could see them better—see how some of them heaved in the water. Barataria Bay. Tugs, barges, shrimpers with

237

their skeleton dredging apparatuses like beat-up wings, like pigeons after cats got to them, then petrified in rigor mortis. Stiffness was what they all had in common, stiffness and rust. I pulled the oars in and we continued in the same direction. Just like I figured would happen. We were caught in the resin's wake.

The guy told me it would happen. The one who contacted me. But now he was nowhere around. Not only him, though, no ghosts were anywhere near there. It creeped me out. All that was there was the circular ranting of Lucius Holt's memory, flashing like cracks of heat lightning. They put his eyes out and hanged him, what they did. They blinded him, strung him up slowly so his neck wouldn't break, so he'd hang there and bleed awhile before dying. Vidrine must've seen some, too, he said once, terse, matter-of-fact, "Lucius Holt."

Maya didn't say anything but, she turned around and shot me a wild look, a rapturous look, flashing eyes like a kid in the army, first time seeing combat, first blood, turning the fear into thrill. About fifty yards off, our little boat picked up speed, like it was a fishing pole being dragged around by some big invisible fish, we could only wonder. We were being threaded into the face of a particular boat that loomed apart from the others and heaved and creaked more than its neighbors, sucking up mud from some gash in its underbelly and letting it roll and spill off its rotting deck. The whole boat will one day be Tchefuncte, which will one day be Mississippi, one day all will be one with the stinking source. Is that where I'm going? Is that what the headless man wants? But why?

Maybe my blood will free Lucius Holt from his private hell, I wouldn't mind. It hurts even to breathe in the same space with him, he shouldn't exist anymore, not like this. They caught him looking through the wrong window. Far as I can tell, it was just some lady he was supposed to be delivering groceries to. But maybe, maybe, there was sex after the delivery? That's just a maybe. He might have just thought about it. But he was free after that, walking down the road he came down with the empty basket. Sun setting. Getting cooler, I took off my shoes so my feet could feel the soft dry cool dirt of the road at dusk. Then he was with some black woman, maybe his own wife, she had a baby and then she left and he took the baby. Was going somewhere. Probably some relative. Or the lady wasn't related, was just watching the baby. Maybe he was going home. He was walking down some road with the baby when they pulled up and got him. Then he was on this boat *jeepers boy you got some peepers.* Bigger than most of them, too. The boat. Some kind of pleasure ship. Like an old steamboat, not a real one though. Like the Mississippi Belle, a fake, but an older fake. They had dances on it, once. Gambling. Hos. Illegal drinking. When Holt was on it the paint on the wooden trim and fixtures was just starting to peel. It was a dull green color. And a door still opened and closed, but it always slammed shut because the stern stuck up out of the water at around a twenty-five degree angle. (It's settled closer to earth by now, the whole structure has melted and crumbled over the years). Holt looked up from where he hanged, trying to grab onto something with his hands, and saw how the raftered ceiling they hanged him from wasn't straight over his head, but at a slant. And baby wailed and was cussed at and threatened, too, and he hoped he was too young to understand or remember and then little Rafe was quiet, or else he was dead, himself or his son, one of them, he knew he was too young to be a daddy and this is what he got for not running off. He got pissed. They unstrung him and let him rest some more before they did the whole thing over again. At some point they dug his eyes out. Some guy did it with fingers. At some point he got pissed again and died and got busted by whatever was looking down from heaven.

Charles Cannon, from Soul Resonance: A History of the Great Rift and Its Consequences for the Living and Dead

Despite four separate and exorbitantly funded efforts over the years, the physical remains of Alphonse Clouet have to this date not been located. Nor has the shade of Jessamine Bascomb, which project has also drawn the best psychic energies around the world. Undoubtedly, the stubborn silence of Rafe Vidrine and Maya Vracar is a prime reason for the failure of both objects. In the two years since Vidrine died at his home in New Mexico (at the age of one-hundred and five), a new wave of financial enticement and legal intimidation has devolved solely upon Maya Vracar, but she continues to be tight-lipped regarding November 23.[4]

---

[4] As the reader will recall, during the hysteria following the Rift, Congress passed the Citizens Responsibility Act, declaring it unlawful to withhold information on an issue deemed to be of vital national security interest. Rafe Vidrine was immediately tried under the act, but when the case appeared before the Supreme Court, the CRA was struck down as unconstitutional (by a scant 5-4 vote). As of the date of this publication, a similar bill is being brought before the House of Representatives.

241

However, at least as to Clouet's body, the mystery dates considerably further back than the Rift. After his execution in 1877, he was laid to rest in St. Roch Cemetery, but did not rest long. His mausoleum was broken open and its contents robbed within the year. As Rafe Vidrine tells it in *Beyond Yellow and Black,* the corpse dangled the following morning from a lamppost on Canal Street. It was removed by police and supposedly reburied. Rumors abounded as to the inability of the corpse to stay put. Clouet's former colleagues claimed actually to be in communication with his spirit. Clouet had been a member not only of the integrated French Scottish Rite masons, but of a spiritualist society comprised of many of the same persons. Records of their regular séances survive, though not from the period following Clouet's death.

At any rate, one of the first official actions inspired by the Rift was a court order authorizing the exhumation of the Clouet mausoleum. It was found to be empty.

Jessamine Marie DuClous Bascomb

My Spring Queen abdicated and flew into exile. Like the glow of an extinguished lamp, like a favorite book of verse long misplaced. To Europe, I have no doubt. I thought also of fleeing back to the Old World, but found with some alarm that I did not have the means. I became an unhappy hermit. I lost my taste for society. That is to say, the taste of society itself had grown sour. I remember only a single social call from those encroaching autumn weeks which would serve as my twilight.

Of all the extraordinaries Clara Reina and her brother introduced me to, the acquaintance which would prove most decisive was that of a certain Madame Amestris. She enjoyed high repute among the ill, lovesick, vengeful, and threadbare. She was rumored a descendant of the Tchoupitoulas, and learned in the ancient arts of herbal alchemy. A *voudou*. She was adept at mixing all manner of potions, whether to soothe the mind or to inflame the baser instincts. Only once did I call on her unaccompanied. I took the Rampart streetcar far out into the third district, where she occupied a humble but well apportioned cottage, an old bright yellow stucco affair, slope-roofed and fast against the narrow turf walk,

243

back of which grew her secret garden. She waited in her open batten doors as if she had been expecting someone. She claimed, of course, that it was I she had been expecting—wiles of this sort belong to the trade of such women. She wore the customary immaculate white *tignon* and a less immaculate stub of clay pipe in her mouth, and spoke the *ancien* and corrupt French of her caste. There were two great magnolias on either side of her abode, and the sweet acrid scent of the red berries, crushed underfoot, filled my nostrils. The velvety cones littered the bricks of the *trottoir* at the side of the structure. She did not invite me into her home, but rather ushered me through a narrow side alley overhung with the velvety pods of sleeping wisteria. I fancied that the great festival of scents was in celebration of my latest sudden resolve. I imagined that the bees in the honeysuckle were sprites playing upon great bugles, and that the wafting mosses hanging from the live-oak in the rear yard were banners heralding a glorious eternity of perfumed mists and gently cooling sprays of rain. Madame Amestris took my hand and sat me at a wrought iron table situated between her garden and an open stable which housed no beasts, but served rather as her apothecary. There were shelves upon shelves of miscellaneous jars, bottles, little wooden boxes, and great clay urns. She served me a bitter-sweet *tisane*, with bits of what appeared to be tree bark floating in it. But my tongue soon grew accustomed to it, and soon as she perceived this, she said, in a commodious way, "*Alors*, Miz Jez'mine, why you come 'ere?"

"I should have thought you'd know, given your peculiar abilities." I immediately regretted my ironical tone, but the truth is, it has always leapt out of my mouth before my mind could ever get the reins on.

Clouet once announced his suspicion that this was
the case and I forthrightly agreed.

"All I know, you come 'ere to gid somethun' you
'shamed to gid."

There was a topaz glinting in her eyes which caused
me to hear distant harps and flutes, and made me instantly
trust her, yet still I felt compelled to lie, for her own
sake, I told myself.

"My mother," I explained, "is greatly afflicted...and
in much pain, she suffers so."

At this her toothless mouth erupted in a great cackle.
She put her hand upon mine once again and expressed
her doubt that I had seen *ma mere* in many a moon. "You
a beautiful chile," she added. "Why you wan' dat?"

I replied that I was in confusion as to whatever she
might be referring to. She shook her head and wagged
her finger. "You in the wrong place."

"Yes!" I cried, for she had diagnosed my ailment
perfectly. However, she then advised that what I sought
could best be obtained from a *pharmacien Americain*. She
said she heard tell of a place Uptown that could well
serve my intent and I could not suppress bitter laughter
upon hearing the name. In Jackson Avenue, *Pope's*! I
found it too fitting that the lair of my father and his associates should serve to book my passage.

I took leave of Madame Amestris and embarked on
a most retrograde journey. I had not been above Canal
in years—I shunned it just as my mother shunned the
French municipalities after her marriage. My discoveries
there took me unawares. For the contrast to one accustomed to the creole districts was most striking and most
sobering. A great cacophony of hammers and saws and
the shouts of workingmen greeted one from the river-
side of St. Charles Avenue. On every corner a great manse
was being erected to outdo the ostentation of even the
boom years before the war. I had read in their papers of

great hardship and privation, yet of these nothing was to be seen in this quarter. I had assumed that the entire Isle of Orleans sadly drooped in her joists as did the domiciles and dwindling commercial places below Canal. The white creoles never tired of blaming the war for their decline in fortunes, yet, here, along the broad, straight lanes of Washington and Jackson Streets, were all the signs of a buoyant prosperity. I began to send out questioning scouts to all corners of my doleful mind, yet none returned with a fruitful report. So I was left with my previous resolve, only more fortified.

As the little bell rang at the door of Pope's, I drew the veil over my face and made careful to speak in hushed tones, lest I be recognized, captured by the enemy.

Rafe Vidrine

By the time our boat nudged the body of the wreck, I knew I had been there before. I knew Lucius Holt was more than a name I had come across in print somewhere. It was he who had given me my life's ambition—to find him and to find out how he had come to the end he came to. My whole career had been a great circumlocution around this one moment. This is why I couldn't bring myself to stop Mills. Also, no one stepped forward and asked me to anymore. Jessamine Bascomb was far away, I assumed she had given up. I didn't realize then that it was too dangerous for her to come near. I know now that Maya Vracar had many of the same doubts that hounded me, but all we did then was trade conspiratorial glances. We both burned with the same pathological curiosity—to see what none had seen before—yet we both wondered which of us would fall victim to Mills' grand plan.

He stood and placed his hands on the resin ship. He bowed his head and said, "Yes, yes." Then he spoke to me. "Vidrine? You got any writing left in you?" I said I hoped so.

He asked Maya what she planned to do with her life.

She said, "Live it."

He laughed, "I might be living mine still," then abruptly stopped. "But I don't know."

The rotting ship jutting up backwards out of the water had begun to tremble. Mills put a hand on it again. "It's like a sleeping dog dreaming about chasing a frisbee. Somehow this object knows something." He grimaced as if faced with an unsolvable math problem. "We might be getting screwed here, OK, y'all? I have no idea what's going to happen." He seemed to want to laugh again, the corners of his mouth strained always just short of smiling. "Does that surprise you?"

Maya nodded and I shook my head.

His next question took me off guard: "This Clouet. What kind of a guy was he?"

I paused long enough for him to wonder about the irrelevance of his question, but he didn't add or subtract anything. So I bumbled out an answer. "I don't know. It's hard to say. An opportunist. Committed to some vague image of progress, though not a systematic one. A pragmatist, probably. Driven by more than just a narrow class interest—"

"Nice guy?"

Neither archives nor Jessamine had answered that question with certitude. "I wouldn't be able to say. Seems like he may have been, but who can say?"

Maya piped up, "Who is he?"

I described him as a "nineteenth-century political figure."

Maya asked Mills why he cared.

He said, "He's out there."

"Aren't they all?"

"Yeah, yeah, Maya," he mumbled. "Reach in my bag and get me that knife."

While she dug through his bag, he began removing his clothes. First his magnificently filthy plain white business shirt—the streaked stains were a vast enough history, but indecipherable. He removed the shirt one slow button at a time as I tried to read the language scrawled on it by his recent experience among us. He unbuckled his belt, let his pants drop, and then worried about getting his shoes off. He said, "They should've just kept these." I don't know what he meant by that.

He took the knife from Maya and looked at it the way a child would look at some hated food. Then he commanded that we close our eyes. Maya and I looked at each other first, then she closed hers, and I mine. But I no longer feared for either of us. Mills was the only one to fear for, but I refused to fear for him either. Over the breathy, beery drone of the resin, I heard him get out of his shoes and pants and drawers. Then he said, "Well, here goes," and I heard him splash into the water.

We both opened our eyes and watched him swim around in small little laps a few yards from the boat, the knife in his teeth. Then he went under and came up again where the ancient mossy deck listed into the water. The knife was in his mouth and he was completely naked. His body seemed to reflect the moonlight like a fish just below the water's surface. He walked upward, astern, up the slanted deck, leaning forward to keep his balance. The boat purred evenly, as if an engine were tucked away below. It made the water droplets sweating on the green rotting steel buzz and reflect like diamonds.

A great swell kicked up. We and the junkheaps around us sloshed around in the wake of some giant invisible tanker. The groaning of the soul resin began more and more to resemble a hoarse human voice. I almost blacked out from the pain it inflicted on my raw ears.

Then perception seemed to slow down as its focus became more complex, like the memory of a car

249

accident. At some point Maya and I both stood and prepared to board the resin ship. We groped at the wet rust of its unnatural exposed underside, but Mills shouted at us to stay put and we both did. We were both frightened, out of our league, and of no use to anything but after-the-fact history.

Mills paced around for a few seconds, as if trying to find some exact location. He finally stopped and stood still, and I saw—or thought I saw—above his head, a gray swath of ancient rope rotting in tandem with the old wooden beam it married seventy-five years ago. Then Mills apparently lay down, maybe sat, we couldn't see. We heard a muffled grunt from him. The drone markedly intensified, up in volume as well as speed: that is, pitch. It leaped suddenly from its bass to the heights of audible range, then beyond. The stressed metal of the resin ship bulged like an overpressured steam valve. We saw a dark trickle creep over the side of the deck and slowly descend. When it hit the water, for the first time in history, all hell broke loose.

November 23

April Brunnen

I stopped missing you when the wind started trying to tear me up like I was a piece of newspaper in that
old "ginsu-knife" commercial, it was like before the dream,
then it was guys, this time it's like everything, it's so hard
to stay together, it's like going back and forth on a cheese
grater that goes right through you everytime. Jessamine
says we need to keep fighting against the wind, we have
to keep walking right into it *they wish us gone, ma chérie,*
they have no use for us and wish us destroyed
and I didn't even think I was the same us as her but
I guess I am, we're in the same boat and it's against some
big current. I feel like we're walking into a fan, and you
can see how other people like us aren't making it, first
they stretch out, and their mouths open up screaming but
you can't hear them and then they break into like little
pieces of liquid glass and then they're just this white cot-
tony stuff that's everywhere and always washing back
toward whatever's behind us that Jessamine won't even
let me think about checking out *you are more prepared,*
brave April, yet I have forgotten how to die, I fear what
terrors may lie in this next brutal mischief played upon the
soul's expectations, I want now only to visit with you a little

longer I'm dead, that's what happened to me. I don't even have time to grieve about it 'cause now I have to worry about this new shit that Jessamine says isn't normal at all. There's this sound in the gales like a DJ messing around with a Robert Plant riff, from one of the trippiest druggiest *Led Zep* acid jams, like when Bonzo's not kicking out a beat anymore but just freaking with the cymbals and Jimmy Page is chewing on the e-string instead of playing it. Everything's coming up drowned, everything's like stuff floating up to the top of a river from a dredging and everything's bloated and wrong, like the way I feel, the fact that I feel at all *Is this feeling? To me it is dyspepsia, though my extremities tingle as they did once waking from sleep*

The other people can see us, I can totally tell, the other people are looking at us, the live ones, fuck them, they shouldn't look, don't look at me *Yes, dear, they see us—they rapidly join us too. They regard us with such disgust and contempt that they hate themselves for looking, though turn away they cannot, so they join us, these fools who know not death, and they are the resin's easiest prey for they have no strength here, they are like the sad man who awakens under water, finding hand and foot bound*

Where's Mills? Jessamine, where's Mills? Is he in the resin, too? *Your Mills is the cause of this catastrophe* Oh, bullshit, you're always saying gloomy stuff like that. There's a guy that's never seen a naked girl before, see him checking us out?

"Can you hear me?"

Yeah, sure, I can hear you

"Where are you going? Can you hear me?"

He's following us. I don't want him around.

"Are you all right? What's happening?"

I'm dead, so uh, not all right, capiche? I think he heard me. He's not running after us anymore. He's just standing there getting washed over by the other ones.

He's trying to flick them off his face like they're bugs or cobwebs or something.

Mills Loomis Mills

Good aged blood doesn't smell like death. It doesn't even smell like the filthy Mississippi. It smells like the sun on the grass, on pine-needles from the little *piñon* tree before it becomes tumbleweed. It smells like New Mexico. Like April's hair.

Charles Cannon, from <u>Soul Resonance: A History of the Great Rift and its Consequences for the Living and the Dead</u>

Shortly before dawn on November 23, something like snow began falling on New Orleans. In texture it was more like ash, but chill to the skin. Something like thunder preceded it. As the rumblings came nearer and got louder than clouds had ever before been known to, people started anxiously out of their beds. When the dawn failed to arrive, people checked their clocks, prayed, wished they had basements, began earnestly drinking, and loaded their weapons.

They soon realized that the strange new phenomena of sound, smell, and climate had little to do with weather. The general smell has been described variously as rich soil, bottom growth woods, rust, blood, and old semen.

The sounds were more intrusive. After a point, the threshold between simple noise and acute, uncomfortable, bodily sensation was crossed. It struck the ears and entire body, a slow ripping sensation, like sawing through dense cardboard, or even sheet metal, or the earth's crust itself, though no seismograph registered anything. It was also described as a beach grated by stormfront waves, a chorus of foundation pounders, a crowd of spectators ooh-ing and ah-ing in sync with each other.

Those heavy sleepers who were finally wrenched into wakefulness saw flickering lightplay at their windows, lightning filtered through a strange-colored fog. The reverberating breathy pulse saturated them to their bones, causing migraines, causing many to faint. The physical experience was so intense, and came on so suddenly, that many feared stroke. Some reported paralysis. Almost all complained of a debilitating dizziness. A medical student recorded her impression of being stuck inside a great artery, obstructing bloodflow in a colossus straining toward cardiac arrest. An understanding of the streets as a clogged circulatory system was related by thirty percent of those interviewed. The precipitate in the air was far denser than water and its taste, like rust, led many to fear an explosion had taken place at one of the petrochem plants outside town.

But when they looked to the sky for signs of fire, their apprehensive confusion became the murderous and suicidal rage Nov. 23 is now remembered for. Swooping down on the city they saw layer upon layer of purple and crimson sheets, woven from a cloth unlike any they had ever seen: a molasses of flailing limbs and howling, terrified human faces.

Rafe Vidrine

I now know what it feels like to be in more than one place at the same time. Of course this changed my outlook on life, and has affected the texture of my experience from moment to moment ever since. The last thing I remember from "before" is sitting in our little aluminum fishing boat, looking at Maya Vracar, then taking the hand she reached out to me. There followed a few seconds of a kind of peace that comes from expectation of unprecedented catastrophe. I squeezed Maya's hand, felt the gentle rocking of our boat on the quiet water, a light breeze, heard our boat's nose bumping against the old wreck Mills had boarded. A voice cried Mills' name (I suppose it was Maya). A red burst as if from an old photographer's flashbulb cued the Rift. My mind seemed to stretch like saltwater taffy, one end seemed at first well grounded in the boat, while the other rushed into a powerful vacuum up where Mills was (or had been). Maya Vracar and I went through this together. We went through Mills. In the process we became intertwined ourselves. So I can say I know what it's like to be a woman, though not what it's like to have a woman's body. We didn't exactly "leave" our bodies, but their

forms became reduced to the mere fact of flesh. We kept
our flesh, but for a time I think it was condensed around
our consciousnesses like the earth's crust wraps around
its core. No limbs, hair, teeth: just a stew of the basic
ingredients of flesh and bone. Eyes? We saw, so we must
have had them, but I believe now that the entire surface
of whatever we became was eye, nose, ear, and fingertip.
Or else it was all palpable illusion originating in mind.
The red flash became red dust which soon settled into
red air and red sand. Then forms appeared—human forms.
Before I could see, I could feel, in a place like my heart or
stomach, panic, rage, the impulse to vomit, and, in a distant whisper, a strange form of lust. This complex traded
places with a breezy—and cedar scented—contentment.
Like love. I could still feel Maya's hand, and when the
love came around I felt her sending it back to me, we did
it together. The other sensation boiled down soon to a
pure form of pain. It felt like my teeth, wherever they
were, breaking under a scrap of iron. At these times,
which began more and more to end in brief blackouts of
consciousness, Maya's hand became a claw, burning red-
hot iron tongs.

What we saw was rape, in a patch on red sand with
a gorgeous but scary red sunset churning around it. But
it was two rapes. The men changed, though the number
(three) and placing, positioning, stayed the same. The sil-
houette would be the same. The only difference, besides
the changing face of one of them, the only face I saw,
was that sometimes they were dressed the same—uniform—and sometimes not. With every last shred of will
I could muster I held myself at a distance from that picture. Maya did the same. We weren't separate. Both she
and I, in our rattled unison, desperately willed not to see
or feel the victim any more than we had to. So I don't
know what the victim looked like. Without doubt female, though—this much must be reported.

Our first instinct was to leap back, justifiably, to run away. We managed to whip ourselves back to where we thought our boat should be. But we found only another horrible scene. Only this time I recognized someone. Then I recognized them all. Rafe Vidrine recognized them from submerged records of infantile memory. Lucius Holt remembered them from a visceral present. Again the number was three, again they appeared frozen in attitudes of motion, like the red desert sea behind us, but here the environs were a damp dark green and brown. The sky flowed softly and deeply by. The things inside me that throbbed like my teeth, they didn't shatter, they pulled out slowly. They pulled out so slowly that it was *almost* not pain, but merely the memory of pain. I saw me, baby me, and Lucius Holt, my father, saw a vicious hot roiling brightness from where his eyes used to be. But he listened, and heard my cries, and muttered his own. Yet all of this was more blunt, distant, muffled than the girl's experience. It should have hit our inner ears like a smoke-alarm, but the sound of our feeling of it seemed buried under six feet of old, settled dirt, and grass. I would have been happier remaining there, but Maya, confusing her thought of my feeling with the veritable item, whipped us back forward into New Mexico.

There it was the same. Pain like jabbing at recently de-toothed gums, but in there somewhere, buried within the pain was this love-like peace. We strained in the direction of the non-pain, obviously. As we did, the brutal tableau grew more hardened and began to lose color. What had appeared to be stiff human forms engaged in a decipherable act began more to resemble stones, stone monoliths. The red gave way to a glistening black. Then the churning at the borders of the scene moved toward the center and we found ourselves spiraling into a kaleidoscopic formation of black crystal. This ended in an unconsciousness we were both sure was death.

Jessamine Marie DuClous Bascomb

I drank from the well of night, thinking it would mean sleep. Silly notion! Thus the living grope blindly about their bright days in search of palatable shades of death. It were better had they wasted no thought upon it, for the energy they expend is just so much waste. My little bottle, my blue vial of hope, my listless lover, how you betrayed me! Your gift contained pillows and arrows alike, for I while away my tedious eternity with visions of Reina as well as plentiful bitter draughts of the others, the ones called men. And myself, of course, who for a time became the plaything of a man. My unrightness in the world made me think to nap for a while and wake up in another time. Ah, *c'est ca oui,* and that I did! Though I awoke only to see but not touch, and the world remained largely as it was, still, how do you call it, darling? *Shitty, a shitty place.* Indeed, a shitty place. Though our memory of it is often lovely. *I don't like my memory.* You lack the practice, and patience, to discover its proper usage. *Blah blah blah, where are we? Use your brilliant fucking dead brain to figure that out.* Precisely why memory offers a more pleasant haven. There is nothing here to see but millions of us. All we want is free room to wander alone and here we are tormented by this, this unwholesome *tiraillement*, this crumpling of our terrain. *But I don't feel the pulling anymore.* Be assured, it continues to peel away our outer layers, it is still active. I feel trembling in our ranks. I also sense that we have been summoned here through some grand scheme. I am haunted by premonitions that I know its author. *You said it was Mills.* No, no. Someone else has corralled us here. One of our own.

Rafe Vidrine, from Beyond Yellow and Black: Franco-African Political Culture in New Orleans

On 14 September, 1874, Alphonse Clouet's second death-knell sounded. An armed detachment of the Crescent City White League (numbering over three-thousand Confederate veterans) staged a coup which displaced the regime of legal Governor William Pitt Kellogg. Within a week, federal troops would re-instate the governor, but the blow dealt to him, Clouet, and Reconstruction itself, was mortal.

The summer of 1874 was perhaps the tensest since 1866. A primary difference is that, while 1866 was a matter of the white supremacists' testing the waters, 1874 came after a growing campaign of terror against blacks and progressive whites (waged mostly in the countryside, far away from federal garrisons). The Crescent City White League had come out of the closet in 1874, openly promising—and practicing—assassination, disruption of court proceedings, church burnings, and torture, in their avowed bid that "The niggers shall not rule over us." On September 13 a boatload of guns arrived at the foot of Canal Street to help finish the job. When Gov. Kellogg refused to allow the ship to unload, the Confederates cried that their inalienable right to bear arms was being infringed upon and, quoting that "sacred instrument," the Constitution of the United States, called for more armed insurrection the following day.

Clouet, under the command of former Confederate hero (now debased Scalawag) Gen. James Longstreet, deployed his division of the black State Militia in front of the U.S. Customshouse. Across Canal Street, on the Uptown side, ranged the White League forces.[5] Under cover of a slow-moving freight train, the White Leaguers sneaked close up to the unsuspecting government forces and suddenly opened fire. The advantage of surprise helped make the conflict short and decisive. After about fifteen minutes, eleven members of the Metropolitan Police lay dead and the rest, along with the State Militia, were in headlong retreat. Clouet was among the scores of wounded and most likely would have been lynched on the spot had he not quickly been spirited away by his comrades-in-arms.

Once again Clouet had escaped the death-squad. Not so many of his subordinates, however. Many were captured, stripped of their uniforms and beaten. The fact that there is no record of a killing in captivity means only that no one thought the matter worth reporting. National news sources had also tired of reporting always the same story from the south. Many northern papers (including even formerly pro-Reconstruction voices like *The Nation*) sided with the White Leaguers. For northern progressive whites, compassion fatigue had set in. As for southern blacks, they had been dying

---

[5] Among them numbered one Edward Douglas White, who would later make the U.S. Constitution more amenable to his class as a Supreme Court Justice voting with the majority (against the radical Creole plaintiff Homer Plessy) in the case of *Plessy vs. Ferguson*.

in such numbers since the White Terror began in 1868, it became exceedingly difficult to keep up a reliable count. Clouet, however, proved hard to get to—unless, of course, legal channels could be brought to bear. Indeed, within a few years, the White Leaguers' domination would be complete enough to come up with white judge, jury, and executioner, so that Clouet could be lynched with all the blessings of judicial procedure.

Rafe Vidrine

It never occured to me to look for my wife at the next place we got to. Of course, apparently not everyone stays where they fall. But I didn't even think to look for her. I didn't exactly "think" about anything. When Maya and I "woke up," we found ourselves in the midst of a huge crowd. I attempted to move—just my head—and found I was paralyzed. We looked at each other in stark fear. She seemed more terrified than I was, if that's possible. But we soon regained the use of our limbs and realized immediately that we were different than everyone around us. Yes, they were shades. We didn't dare move, even though we knew our legs worked, because it seemed the crowd was too close-packed to allow it. We were standing on solid ground in the city, on some wide plaza on the river downtown—I didn't at first recognize it. I don't know how long we stood there, hunched, impossibly striving to avoid contact. Finally I saw Maya, brown eyes wide and glistening, lift up her arm slowly, to full extension, and wave it around. It moved in and through these sad and clearly frightened...people. How to describe them? In a sense they weren't "shades." The word implies that a ghost is a semblance of some other, former thing. But these creatures were more than simple left-overs. Their faces were too animated, mouths opening and closing, eyebrows twitching, eyes roving. Their bodies formed out of a general mass of vapor and dissolved again, but never into empty space, always into one another and another. Each anxious to communicate or emote. Or to move, to lunge, leap, or roll (through each other or us). Some rubbed themselves, in evident pleasure, others extended hands in greeting. But as soon as you got acquainted with any particular face, it would implode or wisp away at the edges and become another one. It proved too dizzying, nauseating to look at one space, to watch the rapid fire of new tenant following inevitable dispossession. Better to keep your eyesight general, unfocused, and in motion. Maya and I simply stood and tried to get our geographical bearings (well, I did—I have no idea what she was thinking). Someone bumped into me, and I muttered "excuse me" before I realized that it had to be a living body to upset my balance as it did. I turned and saw a frantic, thin, fortyish white man. Red-faced and unkempt, looked homeless, alcoholic. He was sobbing. "What are *you*, man?" he shouted, face twisted in anguish, and ran back in the direction he'd come.

This must have given Maya an idea, because she took off in a sprint. I ran after her. It was difficult going. Running through them, you could feel them stretching and breaking across your face. It felt like wind in the eyes. It also felt like sloshing through water. Moving slowly, as we had first ventured to do, caused no tactile sensation. You could put your hand in, through the image of a human torso, or face, and feel nothing. But moving faster resulted in a greater sensation of resistance. Also, they didn't seem to like it. I shouted out to Maya to wait, or slow down. She turned around to face me, slowed her

272

pace but kept walking, backwards. Willowy gray human forms spilled to the sides and over her. Judging from their mouthings, they spoke. But I rarely heard a distinguishable voice rising singly out of the blanket of quadraphonic cries, laughs, sobs, and whispers—it was like a dump for the raw materials of human vocalization. Even when an individual voice rose above the tide, it was usually too sing-songy, too rapidly modulating, undulating, to make sense of.

Maya's voice came through clearly and normally: "Are you crazy? Do you think being around all these dead people is good for you?"

No. Yes. I didn't know. "Are you sure it's bad for you?"

She scowled in exasperation and I thought of a better argument. "What choice do we have?"

"Well, I don't like them, they stink."

There was a smell. A musty, animal warmth mixed with a cool earth or stone or iron smell.

"I'm getting away from them, I've had enough of them."

"But where…?"

"They're all around here for a reason, and I don't wanna stick around and find out." She turned to go on and I shouted after her again. She wheeled around once more. "Don't you have any friends?" She seemed changed from the girl I had met only hours ago, but I was changed, too.

"I mean living friends. Don't you have any? Don't you have a wife? Don't you want to see if she's OK?" She had broken into tears. "Don't you know if there's anything wrong with them it's our fault? That if we always stayed close to them, nothing would have happened?"

Yes. And no. Whose fault was it? Which "it"? Were my friends among the living or dead? Where my reliable allies? Maya had taken off running again, but slammed into a curving iron balustrade and fell. She got up, looked at me once more, yelled, with sympathy, "Find your friends!" and that was the last I saw of her. I stared through varying patterns of cloth, chest, chin, and shoulder at the iron railing Maya had collided with. I climbed up onto the railing, still no Maya. I'd lost her. I saw only the ethereal masses and a large round fountain in front of me. And: a colonnade to the left, ferry landing to the right, river behind, sixties (1960s) skyscraper in front—the Trade Mart. The present. I hadn't really been sure but also hadn't allowed myself to worry about being trapped in the past, the hell of my people, anywhere near the front of my mind. I thought of thanking God for the first time since childhood.

I hopped back down and looked at the ground where I stood and then to my right, where I saw the Castillian Coat of Arms, tilework chipping to reveal the brick beneath it. Next to it was the standard of Catalonia. On the other side, Grenada. The blue and white tilework circled the fountain in a gentle curve. I was at Spanish Plaza. After some very difficult thinking (mental function was somehow affected), I decided that since I knew where I was, I could go somewhere. I had just decided where I would go when I heard my name spoken. Who? Not Maya.

"Professor Vidrine."

I turned, slowly, and there she was. Clearer and more stable than the others. She seemed almost... permanent. Her feet, in narrow boots, her wide, rustling skirt. Her hands were clasped together, creamy against the black satin of the dress, clutching a rosary. A black ribbon fluttered behind her head. When my eyes finally reached her face, she offered a subtle, cordial, elegant smile. She extended a crooked elbow to me (as if I could take it). Meanwhile she began to twirl, in her other hand, the rosary, as if it were a boa or a cocktail purse. She seemed at home. I wondered why she didn't seem frightened. As if sensing my questions, she said she feared no longer for her own safety, though she advised me to fear for mine.

I couldn't see why. She snorted. "Have you no eyes nor ears? The bullets fly once more at Liberty Place."

She was correct. There before us, at the foot of Canal Street by the ferry, where the statue of Henry Clay once stood, was the place once called Liberty Place. I heard the guns and saw men shooting.

Charles Cannon, from <u>Soul Resonance: A History of the Great Rift and its Consequences for the Living and the Dead</u>

It is probable that many of the shooting victims were killed inadvertently. In all likelihood, the suicides represented the only successful targeting. The most common pattern was to shoot wildly into the flurry of apparitions, then turn the gun on oneself. An often overlooked fact, though, is that the vast majority of New Orleanians did not react in this way. Many remained in their homes, even though this provided only scant protection from the riotous haunting that persisted for about three hours. Some of those who fled their homes did so for good reason, having recognized someone they hadn't expected to meet under such circumstances. But again, though such instances have been well publicized, they were far from the norm. The vast majority faced a sea of strange faces. Many took the streets with an attitude of gleeful curiosity. In characteristic fashion, many New Orleanians found in the Rift an occasion for celebration. There was widespread looting, but the thefts were confined to food, drink, and only the clothing items and jewelry which could be donned on the spot. Few people considered it probable that normalcy (that is, a "future" in any kind of positive sense) would ever return. Churches were broken into, though not for vandalistic purposes— their congregants were desperate to pray and could not wait for clerical authority. Groups of Catholics administered mass to themselves after forcing the locks on sacristies. A great crucifix was torn from the wall of St. Louis Cathedral and paraded around the French Quarter, where it was difficult to make one's way without treading on the prostrate forms of fearful penitents, their noses pressed to the slate sidewalks. Unlike during Mardi Gras, there were no confrontations between pilgrims and revelers, nor, for that matter, any social contact at all among the various clusters of people who all seemed to share the same hallucination. Survivors later reported that it was difficult to trust anyone whom one did not already know, since one's current associates were the most likely actually to be "alive" or "real."

Perhaps because of this contingency, there was no police or other institutional response of any kind. Mayor Maurice Boissiere, like other public officials, was not heard from until hours after the cataclysm subsided. There were no ambulances, hospitals ceased to function. Fires raged throughout the city (arson was common[6]) with no Fire Department to respond. Most important of all, there was no immediate, on-the-scene news coverage. All we have are a handful of amateur videotapes, none of which show anything other than a "living" rampage.

One of the most comprehensive of these documents, the Gina Frangello tape, starts in Frangello's living room. It stays there, focused on a single, blank spot of wall, for eighteen minutes. Some of the time, at widely spaced

---

[6] Mostly, people torched their own homes, however there were isolated cases of institutions being targeted—a casino and a synagogue, for example.

intervals, Gina Frangello holds up one half of a conversation. Almost all of her statements are questions.

—So why did you come here?

—Was it hard to get here?

—But why here?

—Have you seen me before?

—Where are you from?

—*When* are you from?

At a certain point a second ghost seems to enter:

—Do you all know each other?

—Did you get here the same way he did?

—How long are y'all going to stay?

—How many of y'all are there?

Frangello was less fearful than many. She proceeded outdoors with her videocam and apparently remained calm. She exited her Midcity home at 6:20 AM and walked briskly along Banks Street to Jefferson Davis Parkway, then to Canal Street. From here she continued downtown, toward the river. For the duration of the journey, one hears shouting and screaming, which increases toward the river into a din like the roar of an enclosed football stadium. Most of the tape shows people in flight, simply running.

There are two suicides, however. On the corner of Canal and Gayoso, a man shoots himself in the head with a .38 caliber handgun. From the fifth floor of the Ritz-Carlton, an elderly woman, wearing fine jewelry and an evening gown, dives from her balcony after shouting, "O le plus violent Paradis de la grimace enragee! J'ai seul la clef de cette parade sauvage!"[7]

The river caused the most deaths, however, and presents one of the most inexplicable puzzles of the whole incident. Why did so many flock to the river? Why did

---

[7] Rimbaud. It means, "Oh, the most violent Paradise of the enraged grimace...I alone have the key to this savage parade."

they then so often hurl themselves into it? Some intended to swim, some did not.

Rafe Vidrine

The dead were more and more jostled by the living. Why were *they* here? Now a living mob lurched its way toward the river, many of them shooting. Why couldn't they have stayed in bed? When I asked Jessamine what they were shooting at, she laughed, joylessly. A middle-aged black woman in bathrobe and showercap brushed past me and then suddenly fell. I thought she had tripped, but when I realized she had been shot, I dropped quickly to the ground. It was wet, flooded, actually, with about a foot of water. Jessamine remained still. She looked down at me, wistfully, I thought. She looked suddenly sad, too sad to frown—her forehead wasn't knitted or wrinkled, her face was milky smooth as if in total resignation. She buckled slightly and a trail of vomit, suffused with blood, leapt from her mouth and dripped from her chin. I asked, frantically, if she had been hit. But she was unfazed and returned quickly to the expression of vague amusement she had worn when she first appeared. She stooped and wiped her face dry with the hem of her dress. Still crouching, she seemed taken suddenly by a fresh impulse. Leaping up, she bit her lower lip and said, "I want to see you."

Since she stared right at me while she said it, I
was confused. "Can't you see me already?"

She thought about it, or lapsed again, drifted men-
tally to some other place. She now directed the faint beam
of her eyes past me, to the growing, pushing crowd, who
were far more zombie-like than the dead. They had more
and more to wade through the rising water, yet they
groped onward to the only place the water could be coming from, the river. Jessamine perceived what they were
doing, and was just as puzzled by it as I was. She said,
"Our river will soon have no more room for water. So
much travel tonight. Our enemy, in its brute, unthink-
ing way, has swollen the tide with his rancid angry blood."
She turned her face back down to me. I couldn't stand
for fear of bullets. I crouched close up against the high
floodwall, about a yard from the nearest gate the wide
gate at Canal Street, where the crowd kept streaming
through. "Yet we have, many of us, at least, survived.
Some not. Some dear to us. Now it is you who will pay."

I saw through the gate, and through the fog (that is,
the density of souls) a boxcar on a track. The tracks between Spanish Plaza and the Trade Mart, only I was on
the wrong side of the floodwall. I lifted myself up and
quickly made for the safety of the boxcar. Jessamine in-
explicably stayed directly at my side. But I didn't see her
actually move any limbs. Her method of motion was to
disappear and re-form every fraction of a second, in a
quiet rhythm of water lapping a shore.

She had an easier time getting around the living mob
that was now stopping up the Canal Street floodgate
than I did, though. I had to hug the edge and push
against the tide. The crowd seemed to represent a
strange cross-section of society. All going the wrong
way. The scene was part rock concert, part church
revival (white and black), with a little carnival thrown
in. On top of the floodwall, two second-line dancers

did elaborate numbers complete with twisting leaps. Rising above the middle of the crowd, two people made their way laboriously on stilts. One of them wore a blue wig, the other a tall cloth hat—the Dr. Seuss kind—with Confederate flags on it. I watched one of them topple, the one with the wig, grasping at his side, then stomach. Was he shot? He fell backwards. His head struck the heads of the mass below, but his feet were apparently secured in the stirrups. The stilts themselves moved forward, they were so firmly locked into the tight spaces between the bodies; so the man got dragged along, his head bobbing up and down as the determined passersby knocked it away, one by one. But the wig stayed on. His companion kept moving. Closer to home, my own face brushed against the face of a crying woman, a very young plump white blonde woman. She made inarticulate sounds of fear or rage but didn't acknowledge me particularly. When my head was forced downward, I saw that two different sets of hands groped at her crotch and breast. Someone had climbed up on my back and pushed off of my shoulders to get up on the floodwall, as if I had been a ledge or an old crate. Before I managed to extricate myself from the human stew, I stepped on at least two people. One was a hand, the other a foot, though it was hard to tell because of the rising water. Once I achieved the other side of the floodwall, a rational thought visited briefly: shouldn't the flood-gates be closed? The river was overflowing its banks.

But I wasn't worried about the water, so I guess no one else was.

A few yards from the gate, it wasn't so packed. Like a block behind the parade route, instead of in the front crush of onlookers. Jessamine reformed again. Her forming and unforming was like the furling and unfurling of wings. I lodged myself on a ladder between two boxcars.

I had planned to occupy the car itself, but found other living people already in it. I couldn't trust them. They seemed as frightened to death as everyone else and were just as unlikely to behave responsibly. I heard a great thud above me, very close, and knew somehow from the sound alone that it was a fallen human body. I thought, too, that I could smell the insides of it.

I couldn't see Jessamine, but I heard her voice. "You are on dangerous terrain. You may wish to close your eyes or your ears, were it possible."

"But I don't have to worry about the dead. Right?"

"It is only your eyes and ears they may offend. For myself, I am happily surprised that you don't find my company repugnant."

"Why would I?"

"Oh, I suppose I'm presentable enough. It is my name I thought you might despise."

This last comment presented me with some difficulties. I thought hard. How to explain my take on all the implications she just posed? But I just couldn't formulate anything.

She, however, became angry and visible again. Her finger trembled accusingly in my face. "I could deplore you just as easily, *Monsieur le Professeur*. You have failed. Some professorial dementia has caused you to abet the disaster you, as clearly as I, see before you."

I wasn't sure, yet, that it was a disaster. I was in a kind of shock of scientific detachment.

She continued to berate me, calling me a coward, a discredit to my race, and, finally, a dirty old man. She seemed to feel that my complicity in the whole thing was rooted in a kind of salacious voyeurism. This is when I realized she was probably right in most of her recriminations. She said, "No, you are not one to ravage the innocent, your preference is to spectate. Soon, however, your sensibility will rebel at what you have been so desperate to see."

Then she modulated once again from anger back to a passive depression. She stood again in front of me, and I watched her fidget with her hands. "I have lost again. Befriended and lost. This is the only of life's pleasures I have been allowed once more to endure. , Now I must once more befriend loneliness."

"Who have you lost?"

"Of late I knew a woodnymph. A sprite she was. She has returned to the stars."

"To the stars?"

Her face broke down, and she buried it in her hands and collapsed into a sitting position on the gravel of the railway. "NO!" she shouted. "To the earth. To the pit, as you well know."

For the first time since the Rift began, I felt a deep remorse. Did she mean April Brunnen? To the resin? I couldn't bring myself to look at her or ask.

She began to drift off and I called to her, asking her to stay. She said we'd surely meet again, but that she couldn't stand to witness the travesty that now prepared itself.

I said, "Which?"

She pointed with a fully extended lean arm and then faded away completely. Like dissipating mist. The lights of her gray eyes were the last item to go. I looked where she'd pointed. There, above the swaying souls, stood a form high up on a lamppost, above the crowd of dead. The living were more dispersed here. It seems the living and dead had segregated themselves. This form—of a man—somehow suspended itself from one of the great egg-shaped lamp-bulbs lining Canal Street. He wore a plain soiled cotton shift, and his head was covered with a black sack. He waved his hands turbulently and speechified:

"My well-laid plans have at last come to fruition. I regret that we are brought together by such calamitous circumstances, though history has shown time and again—as we here assembled know better than the living—that calamity, and only dear and dire calamity, has ever succeeded in changing the hearts of the mass of men. I vowed in the moment of my death that, even if heaven I found, or indeed hell, I would claw my way back to the scene of their crimes and make them repent of the stain they blotched our God and Country with forever. They, the living, it is they who torment each other as well as ourselves with their unwholesome delight in viciousness and mean self-interest."

My trance of scientific detachment—or as Jessamine had it, sadistic voyeurism—was greatly increased by this development, so increased, in fact, that I forgot about the clear and present dangers, and left my cover between the boxcars and approached.

I was halfway across Canal when a terrified little man slammed into me and challenged me with a large kitchen knife. It already had blood on it. His hair was nappy—I couldn't tell if he had just leapt from bed without combing it or whether it hadn't been combed in days. It didn't matter. He didn't speak, he simply grunted screeches full of fear and knowledge of the injustice of his plight and lunged at me a few times (inefficiently) with his weapon. He seemed to be saying, "Man, fuck, man, sheee" but I wasn't sure. I easily knocked the knife from his hands and grasped his shoulders firmly. I shouted, "We are in the same boat! We are in the same boat!"

He seemed almost to comprehend. He shook his head and looked as if he were about to say, "Yes, but..." Instead, he wrenched himself free and ran on. Where?

I made it to the base of the tall green lamppost and saw the speaker still held forth. He seemed to dangle. I

shouted the name of Alphonse Clouet. The hooded ora-
tor stopped speaking and almost flickered into invisibil-
ity.

I circled the lamppost, considered trying to scale
it. The base was easy, its seals of Spain, France, the U.S.
and the Confederacy, made ideal footholds. But beyond
this it was smooth and slender all the long way up to
where the staff split into the two curving arms which
held the bulbs. But my attention was soon wrested back
to earth, where a shade was forming right in front of me.
It was first an old gray woman, then a young mustached
white man in an army uniform, then he. The olive-armed
man with the black sack over his head. I asked.

"You are Alphonse Clouet?"

He said, gruffly, "And what matter have you to
press?"

I wanted very much to see his face. "Does it come
off?" I gestured awkwardly at his shrouded head, at a loss
for words, "Can you remove this...shawl?"

He put his hand to his chin as if his face were uncovered, then turned as if waving someone away, "*Quoi
donc! Ne pas possible. Plus tard.*" Turning back to me, he
spoke English, "You must understand, I haven't the influence I once had. Conditions are rapidly changing. Not,
I fear, for the better. I am afraid you and your family
will have to fend for yourselves. We may all have to. We
need to judge our changed circumstances most carefully
and come to our own sound and sober conclusions. *Mon
frere,*" he made to grasp me by the shoulders and his image wavered again when it didn't work, "if you have
the means, emigrate. In Paris all men are equal." He
turned his head from left to right quickly as if casting
wary glances. He was a tall man. A powerful frame,
though slender.

"*Mon frere,*" now his voice choked with emotion,
"the revolution has failed. May God have mercy on

our children." He wheeled away from me on his heels and took one resolute step forward, but then stopped.

The sound of a woman's voice had come from behind me. It called him a name I never came across in all my researches.

"Narcisse."

He stood, didn't move, didn't turn around.

"Narcisse. *Regardes-moi.*"

He turned, slowly. She stepped closer. They stood, facing each other, about a foot apart. She held out her hand, held it pointed down about thirty degrees from her body. He took the hand, lifted it. They seemed actually to be touching. He held the hand up and bowed his head and pressed the hand to his face, as if kissing it. They stood in that attitude (flickering, though, of course) for some moments.

"What have you done, my Narcisse, *ma bête politique,*" she chuckled softly now, "*mon conspirateur.*"

"They needed to be shown. To see conditions as they are and not as they would have them. To know the folly of their course."

"*Eh, bien.* The same folly we knew, yes, and the same from the days of the Pharoahs."

"But they didn't know about us."

"You think not? And did you remember *us*, through all these years of flitting?"

"I have observed you. All my energies have been dedicated to the grand purpose you now see enacted."

"What remains uncertain...what will come of this?"

I was distracted by a danger to the flesh—apparently a bullet. Something whizzed by and pulled at my left arm. There was a fresh jagged tear in my sleeve, warm to the touch. I dropped quickly, splashed into the dingy water. With my hands on the curb, my legs and torso floated in the mild current. Canal Street was becoming a place for gondolas, with a double row of high lamps through the middle, now dark, flanked by the shadowy husks of abandoned-looking commercial buildings from back in the early and middle 20th century. The only light came from fires in second stories. The reflection of flame played romantically on the lapping brown bayou water. It had grown strangely quiet. The voices of the multitude at the river seemed muffled by the rising water.

Jessamine was asking Clouet how he had managed his "crass parlor trick."

"PaPa LeBat?" She whispered, I suppose out of an appropriate sense of discretion.

"*Voudou* is a thing for the living," he replied, "and no doubt of great help in the trivial matters of love and fortune which so occupy them who still respire. However, a higher, more arduous and more scientific regimen must be applied if one wishes to effect sustained contact across the border."

"*Mais oui*...your séances at *l'etoile du nord?* Did these earn you your *diplome d'enfer?*"

"Then I was but a journeyman. One must roam about the night, with no hope of roof, or sleep, truly to become initiated."

"Then we are all unwilling novices. Yet only you have seen fit to tamper with the divine scheme."

"I was sorely mishandled."

"And this your wretched revenge. Those who molested you are now, and have been, here with us. Death levels all."

"Yet the dead kill no one. It is the living who have blood on their hands. You claim that the tyrants of our time have been laid low, as low as the good men of our time. True. But can you deny that their descendants forge on faithfully in their stead?"

"Of what concern is that to us? We left no descendants."

"I will wander in peace with the sure knowledge that at least one great grandson of at least one graycoated monster must suffer on this day."

"Ah, Alphonse, my rash Narcisse, I fear they have long since fled the city, the ones you burn to strike at. They have long been aware that the blood they have shed poisons this very ground. They have fled to greener climes, and left the descendants of their victims to gnash at each other like reptiles. They have instructed their one-time charges well in the principles of brother-hatred, in the notion that one's neighbor is one's nearest extractive resource. If you could assume flesh and move once more among them, they would not heed you. The dream of every descendant of Bascomb's slaves is to be Bascomb, though they have long forgotten the name."

"How easy it is, for some, to dismiss the eternal aspirations of mankind. And how easy for one with the name Bascomb to decry others for wanting to be Bascomb."

"Perhaps I am too hopeless. Perhaps their lives will finally become so long that they need not on their deathbeds always rue their misspent hours. What remains certain, *mon capitaine*, is that it is no longer our matter. You speak of mankind. We are not mankind. I think we, like unrequited lovers, misspend our own time weeping over the mementoes of our lives and resenting the living for their every misstep. Could it be that we neglect too much our own world? Is there a way that we, absent in body and flimsy in soul as we are, can know happiness together, amongst ourselves?"

The water had continued to rise. I had to risk standing because I could no longer feel the asphalt with my fingers. The new bayou was now above my knees. Jessamine ran her hand along its surface, as if she could feel it, as if she were wading out into the Gulf at Grand Isle.

Clouet offered no response, but he took her hand again. He simply held it this time. Jessamine began to fade. Clouet protested, "No! *Chérie!*"

She came back. Her hand was back in his. She said, "Your sister? How is she?"

"She has inquired after you."

"Indeed?"

Jessamine's eyes trained themselves tightly, attentively, on a place beyond Clouet's shoulder. The hooded man turned his head in the direction she looked. Someone was forming there, a shape of about Jessamine's stature. The shoulders, and a wide, full skirt, presented themselves in outline. Then eyes, then a leonine abundance of black ringlets tumbling down over each shoulder, and lightly blowing.

With her eyes still fixed on the new apparition, Jessamine murmured, barely audibly, "Oh, I suppose," her eyes shut as she apparently took a deep breath, "shall we go together for a while?"

And then the trio faded, slowly, and were gone. The new woman had never fully appeared. Yet the glow of her eyes and Jessamine's pointed at each other, floated on the air after their forms had vanished completely. But why, and where, had they gone? I had come to accept their presence as a new fact of nature. I wasn't ready for them to be gone. I had never considered the possibility that they might depart again.

Also where were the others? The air seemed less humid and the great density of soul upon soul had thinned. I saw one here, another there, as if the hour had grown late and only a few stragglers still hurried home. I sloshed for about a block through the veritable canal that Canal Street had become (and so quietly, stealthily). I climbed onto a typically overstuffed garbage can and sat, rested, my legs dangling into the water. The shooting seemed to have stopped or moved further away. I watched the now oddly peaceful deluge, here mostly undisturbed by the dead or living, and watched and heard—from a safe distance— the sea of humanity angrily trying to come to terms with what it had done.

Mills Loomis Mills

I I I I I been duped FUCKING fucked up always
knew I would when it first goes in when you feel it first
stinging on the outside of your skin then swoosh
SHWING it slides right in and your first idea is not it
hurts but how stupid are you "SEE WHAT YOU LOST
WHEN YOU LEFT THIS WORLD" one of April's favorite tunes a big Lucinda Williams fan we were driving
to get little Neshoba we were both singing along with
the tape she was driving Shoba fit in a little shoebox but
what happened to him? I I I I sold him out, too, gave
him away and I remember him watching me from the
other people's porch, like "where you going?" broken
home's all he got, first April then me but April had us
both going to class I said they never expected me to
go she said, come on, be somebody, I'll do it with
you, it'll be fun but I I I FUCKING fucked up AGAIN
and I didn't even get to go to New Mexico, I saw it
and the scenery was cool but then there was April all
dead and messed up gory sprawled on the rocks and
I chickened out at the last minute so I'm still a loser,
the biggest. Shit here it comes around again comes
around goes around it does hurt, really, especially

because I'm trying to jerk it out and that only makes it worse but April and me both know how a knife feels I guess so nobody can say we sold out, right baby? Somebody played me for a sucker—yeah, I know, me, just me, as usual driving around with you and Lucinda and a smiling dog in the backseat is the best satisfaction anybody could hope for I love you.

Charles Cannon, Soul Resonance: A History of the Great Rift and its Consequences For the Living and the Dead

Mid-morning November 23 was compared by one police officer to the day after Mardi Gras minus the sea of plastic cups, beads, without the same overwhelming stench of stale beer. Other Ash Wednesday smells, though, made an appearance. Urine, for example, and vomit.

For an hour or so after the haunting ceased, people simply paused, surveyed, waited. The strange storm had lasted about three hours, roughly from 6:00 to 9:00 a.m. Buildings quietly burned, the fires unmolested. People stared at the blazes but did nothing to stop them, even when their own homes went down in front of their eyes. People sat, heads in hands, on the curbs, or in the middle of Canal Street, in a foot of slowly receding riverwater. Many drains were blocked, sometimes by bodies. Windows were shattered and stores wrecked up and down the thoroughfare, although there had been very little sensible looting. Bodies floated in the river along with many forms of debris, as if a bomb on the docks had thrown bits of warehouse into the water. The greatest crowds lined the levees and docks all over town. They were quiet now. They turned from the river, as if they had sought instruction there, and looked now at each other. Some, looking to their own hands, found weapons (guns, kitchen knives, broken bottles and bricks). Some wondered whose blood, their own or someone else's, stained these weapons and these hands. Many suddenly acknowledged their nakedness, since many had stripped before wading (or leaping from the docks) into the Mississippi. Those who stripped and swam, or drowned, carried no weapons.

City services, with the press, kicked in between 8:00 and 9:00 a.m. Uniformed police appeared and began the massive wave of arrests. Even other uniformed cops were taken in. Everyone in the vicinity of the foot of Canal Street was held suspect. One eyewitness reports seeing a dazed cop who had experienced the whole thing at the corner of Chartres and Canal, being led away and shoved into the back of a squad car by two of his comrades. The National Guard was called out at 1:00 p.m. as more earnest looting and anti-police resistance mounted. Arrestees were confined in the old football stadium, the Superdome. A few unlucky persons were held for days, but most escaped within hours of their incarceration since the police failed effectively to seal the building.

Most survivors speak of an ecstatic sense of euphoria as they realized things were back to normal with the cosmos, that they were, in fact, still alive, and that the dead had gone. This was followed by worries about loved ones. Most people's first action was the effort to locate family and friends.

Rafe Vidrine

I heard Jessamine Bascomb's voice once more that morning, though she remained invisible, maybe even far away. She felt close, though. I thought I could even feel her lips on my ear, though that would have been impossible. These were her parting words: "It is fitting that we should bid *adieu*, since, to all appearances, the world is not, after all, coming to an end." She added, mysteriously, that she would surely call on me again.

But at length I felt a markedly different sensation welling up. It was a pulling, like the abdominal one that had prevailed throughout the Rift, but had started to diminish. That pulling had been nauseating and multi-directional. As if every soul exerted a gravitational force. So, given the multitude, it felt like being stretched apart at the gut. This new tug, though, was fainter, more intellectual (though still palpable). And it emanated from a single direction. If the soul resin's draw had vibrated up through the feet in a heavy bass, this one tingled in a high treble at the top of the head. I jumped down from my perch on the garbage can, into the river. With my feet on the ground, it came almost chest high. It was easier to float. I slipped my useless shoes off. Realized I had been wearing, since another life, a jacket and tie. I let the jacket go, but didn't bother with the tie.

I swam leisurely, grasping here onto a tree trunk, traffic sign, truck's rearview mirror. Various articles of clothing floated along beside me, and empty cans, plastic bottles, styrofoam dishware, plastic garbage cans and chairs, a beat-up umbrella. But the water receded. The flood was ebbing. We were past crest. I dreaded to see what the retiring flood would uncover.

I was soon walking. On Tchoupitoulas toward the Irish Channel, I realized. Then I knew where I was headed. Who wanted me. What other still living person would be capable of making such a call?

As I proceeded along Tchoupitoulas I saw fewer and fewer dead. Light from the sky began to diffuse the cloying, sinewy thickness of souls. I felt more and more rested as I put Canal Street and Liberty Place further behind me. Soon I was in the Channel.

I mounted a porch and rang a doorbell. The house seemed to have made it through unaffected. It was one of my favorite places. Many an evening I had spent happily on its porch, under the frilly Victorian brackets of the awning. With my best friends and with my wife. The door opened. There was Mattie LaVonne. It was her house, after all. She appeared terrorized but intact. I squeezed her close, thrilling almost to tears at the warmth and comfort of living flesh.

But my adventure, my trial, wasn't over. Of course not. The final chapter remained. My own life beckoned, refused to be elbowed out. Mattie, whose husband had disappeared right after the Rift began, sat me down, held both my hands. She might have tried telepathy in the seconds that passed, I don't know. Maybe we were just looking at each other. Soon enough she patted my hand, a signal of resolution, and said, "Rafe, there's someone here to see you." Then I knew.

Jessamine had said my "sensibility" would soon "rebel" against what I saw that morning. And at first it did. Now I saw someone I knew. I knew before seeing her that Mattie had been referring to my late wife, but this foreknowledge didn't help much. In my selected memories I had never conjured up Lauren like this, because this is what she looked like at the end. It was the stuff of my nightmares, emaciated, no hair, gaping, dying eyes. Lauren said I needed to see her now as she is, that I shouldn't sacrifice contact (such as it was) for memories.

I had some painful explaining to do. It didn't require reflection for me to know that I no longer wanted to spend much time in the company of the dead. Yes, this was my wife, but her membership in the ranks of the dead overrode the bonds of affection I'd once felt. The sad fact was I preferred the memories. She must have read all this in my face, because she said, "No, no, I'm not asking for a new chance at some kind of relationship. You're right, that would be sick. I think it would be sick for me as well as you. I've barely gotten used to things over here. Clinging to you would just make me bitter. And it's so hard not to be bitter."

I said I guessed I'd see her over there soon enough. I knew though, somehow, that I wouldn't be over there so soon. I knew a whole new life lay before me, and I was exhilarated by the prospect. But I also knew how cruel it would be to tell such a thing to Lauren. I told her that I did want to see her, but that neither of us knew what kind of relationship a dead and living person could have. "After this moment," I said, "will you be able to find me and appear again?" Already, though, I could barely make her out. She was already almost gone again.

"No," she said, "because it's not right."

I continued sitting in Mattie's kitchen, where we had so often sat before, until I was sure the vaguely surfacing fragments of Lauren's voice or face issued from memory alone. The room grew brighter with sun, and even memory failed me. I called after her, "See you in my dreams." And stumbled out to the porch in search of Mattie.

Charles Cannon, from <u>Soul Resonance: A History of the Great Rift and its Consequences for the Living and the Dead</u>

Neither has any explanation been found for the twenty-three apparent teleportations. Twenty-three New Orleanians—from different parts of the city, having nothing discernable in common—found themselves when the ordeal was over on a rocky plateau in Northwestern New Mexico, near the Four Corners Navajo Reservation. There was no travel in the other direction, probably just because the New Mexico terminus was uninhabited. It is, however, close to the site where April Brunnen was killed. Tribal historians claim it is also the site of a massacre by U.S. Cavalry of a far-flung band of Apaches, but no archive or archaeology has been able to confirm such an incident in that immediate vicinity. All that has been found is sand, scrub pines, shale, and a vein of igneous quartzite.

Dear Reader,

You must promise never to breathe a word of this to anyone until after death. If you're reading this, I've already gone on (back, I mean), so my personal reason for staying quiet isn't so urgent anymore. I am not Maya Vracar. November 23 changed me. I got body, and the body (Maya Vracar), I don't know about. There's probably remains out where Lucius Holt might still be. I guess what I did was "tantamount to murder" or whatever but I'm not the one who organized it, anyway. To be honest, I still don't understand exactly what went down back then and I was such a basket case when I was dead before that I haven't been able to make any sense out of my memory of it. Also I don't want to (remember, I mean). So the only thing I did that was arguably wrong was lie and let people believe I was who I looked like. Good thing, too. If I had told the truth they would've had me in a white room sticking needles in my head. I would have been a brain-opsy and if you don't believe it, you are, as Mills would say, "part of the problem." The way they hounded me and Vidrine anyway. Jail, etc.

Jessamine and I have stayed friends. It would be nice if people would just talk to the dead instead of fucking with them, but Mills was right on that point, too: there are just too many assholes. You can't blame Mills as much, because he was the first, he didn't know what to expect, really (he just wanted to shake things up and he did but he stupidly thought it would make people cool in the future). Now it's just a matter of time. Everybody's figuring it out now. But we're gambling we'll be faster.

You see, cher, Lucius Holt may not be out on the Tchefuncte. He could be, but why would he want to? After the Rift, the dead got extra worried about what misuse of the resin by living assholes could do, and they ("we" again, I guess) have figured out a way to disarm it and free the trapped subject. As Jessamine puts it (she's gotten really big over here), "The unhappy dead toil for Progress. The living squander their most pleasant hours in an unpleasant tyranny of self-absorbtion."